SAY

NOTHING

Carol Bergman

Carol Bergman

Carol Bergman

Say Nothing

Mediacs
151 State Route 32 S #14
New Paltz, New York 12561
www.mediacs.com

Say Nothing
ISBN 978-0-9994664-5-2
Also available as an eBook

Cover design by Chloe Annetts
www.chloeartdesign.com

for all the returning soldiers
may they live with ease

I hope I am not for the killing, Anselmo was thinking. I think that after the war there will have to be some great penance done for the killing. If we no longer have religion after the war then I think there must be some form of civic penance organized that all may be cleansed from the killing or else we will never have a true and human basis for living. The killing is necessary, I know, but still the doing of it is very bad for a man and I think that after all this is over and we have won the war, there must be a penance of some kind for the cleansing of us all.

from "For Whom The Bell Tolls"
by Ernest Hemingway

PROLOGUE

Not long after my honorable discharge from the army, I returned to upstate New York where I had been born and raised. I had been trained to kill by the United States government, and though I had not done as much killing as the other soldiers I knew, I had seen plenty of brutality and mayhem in the streets of Baghdad and Kabul and doubted if my life would ever be peaceful again. When a roadside bomb hit my platoon towards the end of my first tour, I lost nine buddies; five others were badly injured. My brain was rattled, I had nightmares, and was dizzy for a long time after that, but I wasn't disabled enough to be sent home. Instead, I was assigned to another, quieter Forward Operating Base—an FOB in the jargon—where I was in charge of a warehouse. Every morning, outside the perimeter, young men arrived in search of work. They were all barefoot, thin to the bone. I did not understand how they had the energy to lift equipment, or sweep floors, or laugh. But they worked hard and they laughed a lot, grateful for the $5 a day they were earning for their families, I thought. Until I met Anwar. He changed my opinion about everything in Iraq—why we were there and why we were staying there. He spoke only rudimentary English, and because I didn't speak Arabic, I went to the PX to get a dictionary. We taught each other words and phrases as we worked. It was strange that we were so drawn to one another given the disparity in our ages and backgrounds. I wanted to know about his life, how the invasion had affected his family, and he was curious about America and about me, a woman soldier. Why were American women permitted to fight? Didn't I have a husband to look after me? What about my children? He was shocked to learn I had no husband and no children. Why had my parents allowed me to go to war? They had not, I told him. The decision had been mine.

"How can this be, Alison?" he asked me and because it was the first time he used my name, I was uncomfortable and then I told him—roughly—to get back to work. Not for the first time, I had wanted to console him.

One day, my commanding officer noticed that we were talking and ordered me to stop. I explained that Anwar was a hard worker. He was the enemy, the Captain said, and I was not allowed to associate with him in this personal, human way. I was heartbroken but I had to obey orders. I did not speak to Anwar again or explain my actions and, after a few days, he disappeared from the perimeter.

Somewhere in my belongings I have a sketch of Anwar as he is sitting on the floor eating his lunch from our canteen—a hot dog and chips, a can of soda. He might have been fifteen or twenty. It was hard to say as he never answered my questions about his age. He had an exuberant personality. If we'd gone to high school together he might have been the class clown, the kid who was always disarming us with jokes and pranks. He overcame the language barrier with charades and antics. In the context of the war and his reliance on the United States army for security and sustenance, his exuberance was considered unbalanced and dangerous. If he was talking to me, he was breaking the unspoken rules of occupation, and though I had initiated our connection, it made no difference. So he disappeared from the perimeter back into the wretched world of war-torn Baghdad and I worked at the warehouse, equally wretched in my longing for him.

After my discharge, I did not return home right away. I went to stay with a friend in Miami and then I bought a car and I drove north slowly, in painstaking awareness of an intact landscape, of the lush mountain ranges, the trees, the lakes, and the birds. Iraq had been desolate and inert by comparison. Images of dusty roads and destroyed villages haunted me. In Virginia, I visited the parents of my friend, Kate, who had died in the roadside bomb. I told them she had perished valiantly though I did not know exactly what that meant or why I had used the word perished instead of died or killed. Perhaps it softened the loss for her parents and for me.

As I approached my hometown on the west side of the Hudson River, I found a local radio station and listened intently to news about an accused murderer who had recently been discharged from the army. This could have been one of my buddies, it could have been me. How do we stop killing once we have been taught to kill? No matter our childhoods, our parents, the sermons we have heard in churches or synagogues, the Geneva Conventions, or any code of personal conduct, soldiers in a wartime army do not lead a civilized life. We learn how to be practical, efficient and cruel on the battlefield and on the ground we occupy, but we are not kind, and we are not genteel even when we are told to win "hearts and minds." Consider the uniforms we wear and the high-tech equipment we carry: helmets and flak jackets, combat boots and guns. When a child or young person such as Anwar approaches, we must look like aliens to them. How can they differentiate between enemy and friend? Do we raise our guns or turn them to ploughshares? Do we walk off the battlefield or continue fighting? Do we kill a child because we fear he or she may be a suicide bomber? Or do we lower our guns until he blows himself up and our buddies along with him?

My parents welcomed me home with a party which I did not ask for and did not want. I wanted to sleep and I did not want to encounter anyone I knew from my former life except for the

7

closest of family—my parents and two younger brothers. My parents feared that, following my example, they, too, would enlist and they asked me not to romanticize my experience. They wanted their sons to go to college and finish college. The party was a welcome home but, after the party, I was expected to get on with my interrupted life. I had enlisted during my first term at SUNY-Binghamton, the Harvard of the New York State universities. I had always been a good student but what was I supposed to be studying? I can hardly remember. All I know is that I was bored, bored and restless. The army recruiter was handsome and he captured my imagination; I wanted an adventure. When he asked if I had any questions, I had no questions. I signed up that very day and was in boot camp within a month.

What did I know of war? I knew nothing of war except what I had read in books or seen in movies. A distant cousin had been in Vietnam but he had been on a ship. Fearing the draft, he had enlisted in the Navy, so what did he know about combat on the safe deck of his ship? My family and all the families around me knew nothing of war. And I didn't either until I went overseas.

Though I was not sure if I wanted to go back to school after two tours in Iraq and one in Afghanistan—the roadside bombs, the loss of my buddies, and Anwar—I could not think of anything else to do. I had the GI bill and I could live at home, make new friends, find kindred spirits who had been to war and returned from war. I surfed the internet for options and decided to become a private investigator. I wanted to get to the bottom of things, to find the truth, to put the bad guys away. Maybe then the world would be safer and I would be safer also.

CHAPTER 1

I ran into David Rizzo at the art store in Rhinebeck when I was nearly done with my PI training and needed a distraction during exams. Small and expensive, the boutique store in a mostly boutique town had all the essentials for someone in a hurry to get started again after a long hiatus. I had always loved to draw and once thought I might be an artist. A pencil, a pad of paper, a tray of watercolors was all I needed and collecting them into the small hand-wrought straw baskets the artist-owner provided was deliverance. I wasn't paying attention to anything other than the supplies until I saw David or, rather, I smelled him. He was cat-like in his movements and he hadn't bathed in a while. We all become feral on the front but David hadn't washed down, it seemed, and the scent of war was still on him. He was in the store for the same reason I was, he said, and he was glad to see me. When he was a senior and I was still a freshman, we had sketched together in a high school art class, following the trail of the Hudson River painters, and we admired each other's work. I wasn't sure if I liked him personally, though; he hung out with a rough crowd and he was three years older than I was. But many years had passed, we'd both been to war, and our presence in the art store at the same time felt fated. I let myself drift into a fantasy of friendship with him. We made a plan to get together on the

Sunday of that week but our rendezvous never happened. It rained, David called to postpone for another week, then he didn't turn up in front of the Rhinebeck-Rhinecliff train station though the weather was fine and we'd selected a spot along the river to sketch and paint. I figured he had forgotten or that he'd gone on a walkabout of his own. Both of us had seen hard action and what most people consider normal courtesies didn't matter, I told myself. Still, I was disappointed. A day later, his father called me to report David missing. They'd found my phone number above his desk stuck to a bulletin board and they'd recognized my name. I was a girl they once knew when she was still a girl and David was still a boy, his father said. Was I imagining it, or was he close to tears? Had David disappeared before?, I asked. Not for a long time, apparently. But when he first got back, yes, he'd disappear for days at a time, then return home sheepish, apologetic and confused. No explanations were forthcoming, none demanded.

For what seemed like a long time, the police didn't turn up any clues so I went to see David's parents and offered to help. They wanted reassurance, which I could not give them. A soldier goes AWOL from the battlefield for obvious reasons: he doesn't want to die or he doesn't want to kill. Once back home, the reasons become more complex. Wasn't he home safe and in one piece? Why risk danger after the battlefield? Why self-destruct? "His injuries may be invisible," I told his parents. They were smart, educated. I didn't have to tell them this, I thought. Why couldn't they take it in? The answer to that question was obvious, too. Because he was their son.

I'd been interning with a seasoned PI, Margaret Singer, and had the idea we could work together on the case if she would hire me once my license came through. In the meantime, she wouldn't have to pay me. I was certain I could provide useful background information on David and engage the well-honed tracking skills I'd learned in the army. I knew the valley, the mountains, and the reservoirs of the Catskill watershed intimately. I knew some of

David's army buddies, some of his high school friends, his parents. How could I not get involved? True, it would also be an easy way into the profession, a case to begin my portfolio, but that wasn't my only motive: I was scared, scared that war wasn't over for us, that it had traveled home with David and with me in the transport plane, inside our boots or under our shirts, slashed into our skin like a tattoo. We had been tainted, the blood of Baghdad and Fallujah fixed in the follicles of our psyches, as permanent and irreparable as an addict's piercings.

Private Investigator Margaret Singer was fifty-eight-years old to my twenty-something, but we got along well. Her mid-life crisis hadn't lasted very long, she always said; she kept working, she kept dating. Her hair was salt and pepper, she bulged inside her clothes, but she still liked men and they liked her. Peg was her nickname, not Meg, but Peg, she always reminded people. She'd been unmarried for a long time with a daughter about my age but she never pulled maternal on me, only mentor; when we were in the field, we were colleagues. I suppose we might have been taken for mother and daughter. We had a similar muscular build, a jaunty walk, lively personalities, and long shiny auburn hair, though Peg's was dyed. And though we were both moody at times, we were fundamentally happy people, if that's possible, and I think it is. We allowed ourselves moments of frustration, we allowed ourselves levity. The work was difficult, often disturbingly so, and it would have been easy to get whacked off balance. But Peg was steady and so was I despite my months on the battlefield. I suppose that accounts for some of the difference between those who survive and those who don't. It may just be the way we are born into the world, our temperaments and upbringing, or a certain brain chemistry that distills uproar until it becomes bearable. Peg certainly has that steadiness in strong measure. As for myself, I wasn't sure at that time what the war had done to me though, most days, I felt okay.

The development of a neutral investigative persona had been part of the PI training but I didn't know what to make of it because I cared so much about everything I did. Peg found the textbook refrain—don't ever get involved with a client—amusing. She had other, better ways to teach me and when I called to tell her that David Rizzo had gone missing, she didn't hesitate because Private Investigator Margaret Singer has a reputation for responding to distress with compassion. She even lowers her rates, when necessary. We are all under siege at one time or another, she says. Suffering is the human condition. What's important is our connection to one another. I reflected on this wisdom often not understanding as yet where the boundaries were between connection and my yet to be developed professional persona. The town where I was raised, and all others in the counties east and west of the Hudson River, are a neighborhood, families intertwined by ancestry, occupation, or vocation. If we don't know someone, we know of them. Peg certainly knew David Rizzo and she knew his family; his mother, Barbara, was her hair cutter, his father, Mel, her long-ago shrink. Mel Rizzo didn't think that would be an obstacle and so they signed a contract and we got to work.

Though the missing person's report was no more than a collection of unsubstantiated interviews, it was hard to read. It said that David Rizzo was an Iraq and Afghanistan veteran with a suspected alcohol and drug problem. He'd returned from his last tour of duty in bad shape and taken up with an old high school flame, Christa Woolf. I didn't know her well and wasn't aware of the drama in their relationship. She had lived in a trailer with her mother in Hyde Park, David had grown up in Rhinebeck, both towns on the east side of the Hudson River but a trailer park does not compare to the house where David was raised. In high school, David and Christa had hung out in the basements and attics of friends, never at his house. David's parents didn't approve of Christa and said so, the report said. He carried on with Christa regardless. He was crazy about her, he explained to his disappointed parents, just crazy about her. He went to college, she didn't, and they drifted apart for a while, but David and Christa were still considered an item and we all thought they'd eventually get married; high school sweethearts, small town, not an uncommon story. During his two tours—one in Iraq, one in Afghanistan—David wrote love letters to Christa, but she never replied. David said he didn't mind, he understood. Christa didn't like to write, she was self-conscious about her spelling. The two lovers spoke by satellite phone from time to time—a perk of the modern army—but then, suddenly, from one week to the next, David went quiet. He stopped calling, he stopped writing—to anyone. His parents didn't hear from him either. Frantic at times, they also knew that no news from a war zone was good news and tried to live their lives as best they could without their son. He was an only child. The family was a close, loving family. He was in the field somewhere—in danger—and no news was good news, his parents said to themselves every day. I wondered if my parents did the same.

Months passed, David was home, and the couple, David and Christa, was together again and living in a bungalow somewhere in the mountains. Their lives were disordered and Christa was in serious trouble, using drugs, older, out of work. There was a rap sheet on her but David's record was clear. His parents had seen to that. On the winter day that he disappeared, the day we were supposed to meet to sketch, the couple had last been seen staggering out of a local dive, The Eagle. They were in inebriated high spirits, the bartender that day had reported, but David was still sensible enough to suggest they go for a walk before driving home to their bungalow. It was around 3 p.m., the sun already drifting below the mountains. They headed north out of the parking lot towards Annandale, along the banks of the Hudson River. Then, just an hour later, Christa was seen on her own walking south along the same icy footpath, her hat discarded, her bright red hair in disarray, her left cheek bruised. Her car, a beat-up blue 1989 Honda Civic, was in The Eagle's parking lot. She got in and drove away, fast, "like someone terrified," one of the bar regulars had said. She hadn't been seen since though her disappearance had not been reported. That was odd, Peg thought, interesting. Where was she?

I had learned quickly that witnesses under the influence are not to be trusted. Bartenders who don't drink can be reliable and one or two in Ulster and Dutchess Counties were Peg Singer's informants. But she didn't know the bartenders at The Eagle and therefore assumed that whoever initially reported seeing David and Christa in the bar that afternoon and then on the footpath might have missed something. Peg figured that someone had followed them. Maybe there'd been a fight. Maybe some money was owed to a dealer. Maybe another admirer, someone Christa had been seeing while David was in college and then overseas, was jealous that she was seeing him again. Maybe this someone, this admirer, was so jealous he wanted to harm David or scare him away permanently. David might have been pushed into the river or he might have fallen in. Christa might have tripped or David might have tripped. Christa might have been so high that she didn't know what had happened, David so drunk he didn't know who he was or where he was or what day it was. He was supposed to have dinner at his parents' house that night and never showed up. This was unusual, his parents had said. He would have called, at least. Why hadn't he called? I made a list of possibilities in my black moleskin reporter's notebook, a new one Peg bought me as we began the case.

It was winter and the river could not be dredged. It would be too costly to attempt to do so, the state couldn't afford such expenditures, we were told. Either David Rizzo was alive and well or his body would wash up somewhere, sometime, in the spring or summer when the ice floes melted, the police had said. Or maybe it wouldn't. The Hudson River, I reminded Peg, is not a river it's an estuary, water flowing both ways. His body could be washed out to sea, never found, I thought, even though I knew better than to let my mind go to that place, out to sea, say, and then back to the desk Sergeant at the Rhinebeck police station who was cute looking but not very sensitive. "Survivors cannot grieve if there is no body," I said. "Even a fragment of a body is better than no body." I was as expert on body parts as I was in firearms.

"We are pursuing the investigation," the police said whenever David Rizzo's parents had called in the days and weeks following his disappearance. I had been to see them numerous times to emphasize again and again that, contract signed, Peg and I were now advocates for David and for them in the ongoing investigation. Is David dead or alive? Dead or alive? The question haunted, the question seared. Invisible, gone, dead. "There is no way to know that right now," I said. "We have to methodically gather evidence and information."

The cold words burned my tongue. I couldn't wait to find David's body because I was almost certain he was dead. I couldn't explain why the search for his killers might be more important to me than finding him alive. I suppressed that thought until I could not suppress it any longer. When I finally voiced it to Peg, she went silent. Then she said, "Now I understand one thing that the war has done to you. You've gone numb. You're a machine. You've got your eye on the kill."

There was no answer to Peg's insight so I didn't answer. I just kept on working.

* * *

The drive over to Barbara Rizzo's hair salon in Accord on the west side of the river took about forty-five minutes. Peg was driving but this didn't stop her from chattering about first meetings with a client. I realized that in her eyes I was still a rookie and that this perception might be hard to shift. I didn't feel like a rookie. I was a soldier, I had led her to the case, I had already talked to the clients numerous times, Peg was now my partner, my license was in the mail. I would have preferred to talk about my ex- boyfriend or the sales on at the mall because I needed to rest after a night of alarming dreams about black taxis in the desert. Any more of those and I'd have to check myself into the VA Hospital. War turns everyone's life inside out in a different way, I thought—those who go into battle, those who stay behind. And it doesn't matter what kind of family you come from or what country you live in.

I got out of this negative loop by focusing on what Peg was saying. She had a deep voice and spoke clearly. "The conclusion of a case is rarely satisfying," she said. "Are you prepared for that, Alison?"

My thoughts crashed into the first time I had stepped into an armored vehicle. I had no doubt about my mission or its outcome. No doubt whatsoever. This certainty lasted until a group of beggar children approached us for food and money. They ran after the vehicles until they could run no more, their bodies covered with dust, some of them crying, some of them giving us the finger. Where had they learned to do that?

Peg was known for her skill and determination to solve a case but the word "solve" had always bothered her because it was illusory. She didn't say any of this out loud to a client but it troubled her, the sense of responsibility she felt sometimes. Barbara's husband, Mel, her former shrink, would know about it, though. Maybe that's why he had agreed to sign a contract because he knew Peg Singer would persevere until the end, whatever the end turned out to be. I hoped I could do the same.

"I don't think David is alive," I said.

"Don't say that to Barbara or Mel," Peg said. "And, for right now, don't say it to yourself, either. A PI has to stay alert and optimistic, no despair. The Rizzo's loss is not ours. We are empathetic, but we don't get swallowed by a client's sorrow. If we did, we wouldn't be able to work."

For a split second I was terrified I'd chosen the wrong profession, that the steadiness in my nature had been marked by war. But then I looked into the outlines of the mountains against the cloudless sky and I recovered.

* * *

A couple of women were waiting in the plush velvet plum-colored chairs facing the fireplace. One was browsing through magazines and trying to figure out a new cut and the other was complaining that all of Barbara's appointments were backed up. City women are impatient, I thought. I wasn't prejudiced myself but sometimes the sharp comments from the locals were justified. Trailers next to mansions, no work, a depleted economy, a buyer's market, gentrification, city folk buying up all the affordable housing stock for their weekend and summer getaways.

Peg was observing, listening, and taking notes. After nearly three decades in the business, she remained scrupulous. There were legal reasons, of course, but her notes were more detailed than any I'd ever seen. It wasn't a chosen profession though she knew she was good at it, intuitive. Still, she didn't love it all the time. Before she had talked herself out of it, before her husband had left her for another woman and she began her life as a single mother, Peg thought she'd be an artist. So we had that in common, also. Peg sketched in the moleskin notebook. Forensic illustration, she called it. And if she were to admit any regrets it would be that she hadn't become an artist. She envied Barbara Rizzo's ability to make a business out of her artistic talent—she was more than a haircutter, she had an eye and dexterous hands. And she had a sensitivity to a woman's image of herself, what she'd like to become.

I sketched Barbara's down-turned mouth, the sweat staining her thick cotton sweater, heat generated from torment within. All the customers gone, she closed up and made some tea.

"Before David signed up, he was a different boy, a sweet boy," she began.

"I remember some trouble in high school," I said gently.

"What trouble?" Barbara asked her eyes skidding to the Christmas lights on the window.

"I strung those up just yesterday," she continued, deflecting my remark.

She spoke self-consciously, the words dripping from her full lips through reined-in tears. Her large, nearly black eyes were rheumy, the liner smudged. I kept my tone soft and low.

"The lights are lovely," I said traveling for a moment with Barbara into her denial.

"The small ones bring good luck," Barbara said.

"Let's hope so. And let's get to work," Peg said with more force.

I jotted down some observations of the David I remembered from high school, the public image: football hero with the manners of a gentleman, a patriotic fervor, a religious generosity, and a high tolerance for the underdog and the disaffected. What explained his fall, his loyalty to Christa? David's family, all of them, were devout, engaged Catholics with a social conscience. They were the first to volunteer whenever a volunteer was needed.

"We didn't expect him to volunteer for the army," Barbara said.

"Something went wrong when he started seeing Christa, isn't that true?" Peg asked.

Barbara continued, "Mel made a deal with him: Go into the army, let Christa go, and I'll support whatever you do when you return. There was no thought then of a peacetime army becoming a war machine; no thought then of disappearance without return. David did come back after his first tour and he was okay. Not the same, but okay. The second tour in Afghanistan was different. Outwardly, his body was unharmed, but he was hurting. He couldn't sleep, he couldn't eat. His wounds were deep inside his spirit, his heart, and his brain. And though these wounds were invisible, unacknowledged by an official purple heart, they weakened him. He refused to get help. He'd been an officer. We were so proud of him. One day, on an extended stakeout in bunkers surrounding a town, he went to get instructions, just twenty-five yards away, and when he returned all the men and women in his unit were dead, hit by a mortar. David stopped talking, couldn't sleep, and was given an honorable early discharge."

"How did you hear about what had happened?" I asked, remembering my own experience vividly. All I could do was to wait for the pain to ebb. Like David, I had escaped the army unharmed in body and could shut the door on my memories most of the time.

Barbara said, "It was in the papers without his name but his unit was mentioned. And then we got a call from his commanding officer."

Barbara was crying and Peg put her hand on her forearm, told her to take her time.

"David's story is familiar to me," I said. Then I stopped talking. My personal experience might be helpful but it wasn't part of this investigation. I opened my notebook, closed it, sketched the fireplace and the knick knacks on the mantel: trolls, reindeer pulling sleds. Cards on ribbons were looped across the papered walls. As I child and a teen I could not wait for the holidays. Soon it would be Christmas and it was as though it never existed—the days, months and years collapsed since I had signed up for war. I had to make a list and buy some presents I told myself.

"Can you help us?" Barbara asked.

"We'll do our best," Peg said.

Barbara's sobs subsided and Peg said, too abruptly, "Okay, Alison, we'd better be going."

Where are you going?" Barbara asked, shaken.

It was only then I noticed the dimples in her cheeks and quickly drew them.

"The bungalow where David and Christa lived," Peg said.

This was a spontaneous idea. We hadn't discussed it on the drive over.

"I'd like to go with you," Barbara said.

"We have to see it for ourselves, take notes," Peg said.

"I was never invited to the bungalow," Barbara said.

"I understand," Peg said, returning to patience and kindness. The brusqueness was accidental, a detective in a hurry.

"I'll walk you out to the car," Barbara said lingering as long as possible with the glimmer of hope she must have felt in our presence. "We'll leave Alison's car here and talk a bit more when we get back," Peg said.

Barbara gasped as she hit the brittle air, a drowning woman. Which in a way she was; all the breath had been taken out of her when her son, her only child, had disappeared. It might have been easier if he'd returned in a body bag, I thought. But I put a brake on this rumination as I had been instructed by my teachers. I had just been a PI for a matter of days and already these brakes were brittle and worn. I had to watch it.

We got into Peg's car, a yellow 2000 Mercedes coup she had bought from a dealer-friend in Kingston. It was a two-seater with a jump seat in the back.

"I won't head for home until you're back," Barbara said, and even though Peg explained that we might be a while, Barbara said she'd wait.

I squeezed into the soft black leather bucket seat, shoving CD's and folders onto the jump seat behind me and onto the floor under my feet. Peg's car was a mobile office.

Driving long distances on country roads is a time to think and to think things through, put clues together. No music and no conversation, the two-way radio turned down. Another notebook was on the dash, notes scribbled in lay-bys or waiting at a red light. Peg took off her fleece hat and pinned her hair into a plastic clip. "You could use a cut," I said.

"I'll ask Barbara when this is all over," Peg said, words chosen carefully. "When this is all over," not "when we find David," or "when the case is solved."

She was in charge now, deciding everything. I was relieved, more so when Peg said again that David was probably alive, that there was no reason to think otherwise, that it was strange that no missing person's report had been filed for Christa, they might even be together, still alive, somewhere. Another one of Peg's wisdoms: keep hope alive as long as possible. But my soldier's instinct told me there was no hope in David's case and that the truth was a rotten scaffold about to tumble into the woods. In other words, I sensed danger. Whatever had happened, it wasn't over.

I stayed quiet and concentrated on my contorted body in the crammed seat of Peg's impractical sports car. It had already been a long day, beginning with a run in the dark at 6 a.m. my breath beating back at me like a hooting owl. My mother had cooked up cinnamon apple oatmeal, fragrant and steaming on the table when I returned. This gesture of care always cheered me.

I dozed off and then woke to the sound of sleet on glass. We were behind a sanding truck, but even after the sand went down, a slick patina remained on the surface of the road, unforgiving weather conditions. Weather is always real, always manageable in its insistence that we accept the inevitable day to day. Maybe that's why we talk about it so much.

"The car's skidding," I said.

"Hang tight, I'm a good driver."

"I have a bad feeling."

"Let that be. It won't help us right now. I need your sharp soldier's eyes as we enter the bungalow."

The car was low slung and as we turned onto smaller, less tended dirt roads, it lurched and pinged. Tires plowed over jagged slate, ice encrusted trees dipped against each other flinging sparks onto the hood and windshield. Peg angled the car into the holes and slid up out of them skillfully, but it took too long to get there.

The bungalow was a converted shack built in the nineteenth century by German immigrants who had worked in the boarding houses and big hotels in Mohonk and Minnewaska. It had its original pot-bellied stove and sleeping loft, a more recent built-in water closet, a plumbed sink and electricity. The phone had been pulled out of the wall, the two waste baskets emptied and tossed onto their sides like they'd been kicked. Two unsigned sketches were still tacked to the wall. I was sure they were David's. Why hadn't they been taken down by the police?

"Those are David's drawings," I said.

The refrigerator door was swinging on its hinges, the interior wiped clean.

I put on my rubber gloves and popped the drawings into an evidence bag without examining them closely. "These might have prints," I said.

The bungalow had been stripped bare and not by the police. Police don't leave doors and windows open or cracked flower pots littering a porch with dirt.

CHAPTER 2

t had stopped sleeting but the sky was still a lowering gray. The days were very short, dark by 4:30 p.m., the headlights of oncoming cars bursting into view at speed, like flashes of descending stars. Into Ellenville, when we were in cell phone range, Peg called Mel to tell him we were on our way back to the salon and that Barbara would be home soon. He interrupted the message on his machine to answer, his voice strained. "I'll be waiting for her," he said. And he understood, I thought, why she would need him that night. This was assumption on my part as I had not as yet had enough of a long-term relationship with a man to even warrant a hypothesis about the nature of partnership. I studied from afar—my parents, others—enviously. Even in the midst of battle, my buddies all around, I had been indescribably lonely at times. I'd had a fear of psychic isolation since I was a child, before I could name it. I always could identify it in others, especially if the cause was obvious. Mel and Barbara's isolation, set apart from normal families as they sat around a dinner table discussing their day, took my breath away. Their days were no longer average, normal, or sure. And probably never would be again.

I inhaled the air coming through the crack in Peg's window and held tight to the bag containing David's drawings. Peg looked over at me disapprovingly, as though she knew my dark thoughts.

When we arrived back at the salon, Barbara made yet more tea and asked us to sit down, but we did not sit down. We kept the visit short. Barbara wanted to know what we'd found and Peg told her about the empty bungalow. She didn't mention the drawings.

"Are you okay to drive home?" she asked Barbara.

"I'm fine," she said.

We watched protectively as she got into her car, started the motor, and took out her cell phone. The car idled, she made a call, then waved good-bye and was gone.

"Let's get back to the office, take a look at those drawings, discuss what we know so far," Peg said.

I had a feeling that's what we'd be doing for the rest of the evening. I was physically tired and emotionally spent but did not object. I worked for Peg, and if she wasn't shutting down for the evening, neither was I.

Peg lived and worked in a Dutch stone house circa 1670 set back into the woods near Bard College in Annandale very near to where David and Christa had last been seen. She knew the footpath they'd been walking though she had never walked it herself. As a runner, she stuck to the tarmac roadways, mostly in and around the college grounds and the orchards nearby. But as we came up to the house she said she'd like to go down to the river in the morning and if I could stay the night, I'd be welcome. So we worked, stopping only for some homemade three bean soup and spelt bread, fresh out of the oven after rising all day. It felt easy to be there in what had become my office, logical to stay the night. I always carried supplies in my backpack—toothbrush, extra clothes. The army had taught me to be prepared for all eventualities.

We turned the drawings over; nothing was written on the back. One was a portrait of Christa, its' style an homage to Otto Dix, one of David's favorite artists. He was a German who had served at the front during World War I. The trauma of his experiences in the trenches informed his work for the rest of his life. Dix couldn't portray innocence after the war; David couldn't either. His sketch of Christa was more surreal than real, the figure naked from the waist down, eyes wide-eyed, hair akimbo.

The second drawing was a bomb-cratered mountain landscape in Afghanistan. It was as clear and detailed as a digital photograph. Bodies littered the ground around the crater, all of them Afghans in tribal dress. David had scrawled a caption at the bottom in pencil, nearly invisible in the cross-hatched lines: *Bombing of a wedding party.*

"I don't think the police would have left the drawings," Peg said. "They were tacked up after the house was searched as a warning, or a commemoration. We'll hand them over tomorrow. Maybe there'll be an unexpected fingerprint or two."

There is no way to tell if a print is fresh unless an item is examined, prints studied, and then examined again at a later date. So whatever forensics turned up from the drawing would not be conclusive. David's prints would be on them, perhaps Christa's. We had some questions to ask the police about their handling of the site—what they had done— what they had taken with them, or if they had left the drawings deliberately, which seemed unlikely.

We went to bed around 1 a.m. I was wrecked, my body and my brain on overload and I had trouble getting to sleep. My .22 was in my backpack. I pulled the backpack closer and retrieved the gun. Exhaustion settled on me immediately and with it a low-level unhappiness that I was dependent on a small gun as security. I needed to get into better shape—mentally and physically—if I was going to continue as a PI. Much as I didn't want to admit it, David's drawings had disturbed me and, in the morning at breakfast, I told Peg I had changed my mind: David was still alive. The drawings were his signature.

* * *

I borrowed sweats and we went for a run down to the river. Anything was always better than doing nothing my father always told me when he found me daydreaming in my room when I was a teen. I didn't know if he was right any more but the aphorism had stayed with me and, every morning, I set down a series of tasks for the day on an index card and stuck them in a pocket before I ran. No matter how I felt, I ran. At the end of the day, I checked off what I'd done and transferred what I hadn't done to a new card. That was in high school and during the months in college. In Iraq and Afghanistan, as the wailing, violent days wore on, index cards floated in the crevices of the Humvee, flammable tinder, evaporating dreams, illusive goals.

I had two cards in the pocket of my jacket that morning I ran with Peg down by the river, the morning I fell in love with the river again. Though I had supposed I'd settle elsewhere, I knew now that I couldn't leave this place with its rolling hills, sunsets, misty rain, and—most of all—the river, its brackish water white-capped or serene. Suddenly, without warning, the wind might pick up or it might recede, the weather shifting within minutes as it shifted now. We stepped gingerly, adjusted our hoods. If David had fallen in or been pushed in, he would be out to sea by now, fodder for sharks. We continued along the icy, narrow path in single file. Peg didn't believe that David and Christa had been there at all. It was as if the river was opening a door: someone was telling tall tales to detour the investigation.

At last the run was over and we were back in the office. We took turns showering, ate toast and made calls. It was time to make contact with law enforcement, state and local. I struggled with introductions and opening lines; my confidence picked up the longer I talked. Soldiers, by definition, are intimidated by authority, trained to obey orders. It takes a while to alter those neural pathways. It was Peg's job as my mentor to encourage innovative thinking and mine to steer her into a soldier's mind. David would never have risked walking by the river on a wintry day no matter how drunk or high he was—unless he had been forced at gunpoint. Drugs are rampant in the military, even point men use them, which is not to say I ever did, nor that I condone them. I don't. But they are ever-present and the soldiers do their duty high or sober. And they make mistakes, many of them, high or sober.

* * *

The Sheriff's office has jurisdiction within the county, State Police has jurisdiction over cases that cross county lines, which happens often in the sixty-two contiguous counties of New York State. Economic cutbacks in recent years have meant a consolidation of resources and the closure of some small-town stations. Some criminal justice experts argue that police officers and investigators should always live in the neighborhoods where they work, which is what Peg does. Her practice serves Dutchess and Ulster Counties, divided by the Hudson River. Annandale is in Dutchess but Peg knows every road, start-up business, failed business, diner, state forest, and lay- by in both counties like the back of her sun-aged hands. She hardly uses her GPS to get around and I don't either.

"The parents, Mr. and Mrs. Rizzo, came in with a bag of bones," Sergeant De Beyer at the local Rhinebeck station told us as soon as we introduced ourselves.

He was young, earnest, well spoken. He carried an old Dutch name with a long history in the counties, but he had chocolate skin. His ancestors had been landowners, slave-owners and slaves in the colonial era, a rich complicated history. These days, they were politicians, sheriffs, judges and lawyers with interesting last names.

"I don't understand, Sergeant De Beyer," Peg said.

"Bones, a bag of them. I handed them over to the senior investigator, Charlie Griffith, State Police Headquarters over in New Paltz. My name's Ed by the way."

"New here, Ed?"

"Couple of months."

"Thanks, Ed. Anything else?"

"That's it, Ms. Singer. In the future, I'll call you."

"Yes, that would be good from now on so we can work together, move the investigation forward. Here's my card. My name's Peg and this is my associate, Alison Jenkins. We've been hired by the Rizzo family."

"Sorry we sent it over to State so quickly," he said. "But we needed to get a forensic analysis and they're the only ones who have the facilities to do it."

"No problem. I always regret handing an investigation over also, but it's selfish on my part. I enjoy the chase," Peg said.

"I agree," Ed said. "We have less work to do and then they take all the credit."

"Not always. I have a good working relationship with the County Sheriffs and State Police. I hope we can, too, Ed."

"I'm sure we can, Ms. Singer."

"Please call me Peg."

"Peg," and he held out his hand.

There was no coordination at all, everyone working at odds before the investigation had barely begun—no body, no David, no suspects. Why hadn't Barbara and Mel Rizzo called us to tell us about the bones? Were the police obliged to keep us informed? Peg said they weren't, not all the time. But we went to see Barbara and Mel Rizzo to clarify the terms of our contract and to reiterate protocol in person.

* * *

It was Christmas Eve day and the volume of traffic was high as we headed down Rte. 9, an arcade of Christmas lights, to meet Charlie Griffith at the Rizzo's house. He was a senior investigator Peg respected greatly, a decorated detective, astute, and a gentle soul, she said, with a slight flutter in her voice. It was, therefore, no coincidence, I realized, that we were on our way to the Rizzo's in tandem with Charlie's first visit there. I didn't know Peg well enough to tease her about her enthusiasm for Charlie Griffith especially after I'd more than likely signaled my own star-struck appreciation of Sergeant De Beyer. I'm embarrassed to say that I hardly remember our exit from the station, what I said or did. My racing heart took a while to slow down as I drove my sensible Honda SUV behind Peg's impractical yellow sports car. The image of gathering families in the windows of the roadside houses reminded me that I had neglected my own, that I would be late, that it didn't matter to me, and that I hoped I'd see the Sergeant again soon.

As for Charlie Griffith, I'd expected a tall man wearing the classic Stetson, his holster around capacious hips, with a gruff voice and an easy-going demeanor. Needless to say, he did not fit my self-created stereotype. He was tall, he was gentle, he was in plain clothes, and his gun was in a shoulder holster, not on his hips, which were slight. His large round eyes were a striking cerulean blue, and his receding hair was still thick and black. He wore a wedding band which may or may not have been relevant to Peg. The ring was distracting and made me curious about him. I had to re-focus my attention on the investigation.

What a lot of trouble would have been saved if David had never enlisted in the army, his father was saying as I settled into a stiff-backed chair and took out my notebook. Some region of Mel Rizzo's mind has gone into flight, I thought, as he tried to retrieve time. I observed him closely. He was tight, frustrated, enraged. The police weren't doing enough, he said, angrily. He was prepared to sue unless they did more. Then he began to cry uncontrollably.

I couldn't picture Dr. Melvin Rizzo as a normal young father intent on the rearing of a much-loved son, or even as a successful psychotherapist capable of healing others. If I'd met him at a party I would not have wanted to stay near him for very long. But that was unfair because there was Mel before David disappeared and Mel after, two different men. He was our client. It was because we'd been called in that the police were now taking a more active interest.

"You did right hiring Peg Singer," Charlie Griffith said in a tone of reconciliation.

Barbara slumped into her chair and then rose up as if at attention. Her mouth flung open in what I was sure would be a scream. No scream, just a gurgle and, finally, a succinct paragraph: "I want to know how there could be a bag of bones under a bridge right in the middle of Rhinebeck with a grotesque drawing from a putative killer and the police know nothing about it?" she asked.

I wrote down the word putative. Police vocabulary. She must have done some surfing on the internet to pick up that word. Did it relieve her pain? I wondered.

"What were you looking for?" Charlie asked patiently. "What were you hoping to find?"

"It wasn't an archaeological dig," she continued, staccato, her voice shrill again. "The bag was there in the light of day. We went out with the car and stopped at all the places David loved to walk when he wanted to be on his own. We assumed he had a fight with Christa and walked or hitched into town to get to our place in time for dinner. He didn't have his own car. We drew a map and followed his favorite routes. The bridge was first. Mel noticed some graffiti on the inside wall and went down to have a look. It was a grotesque figure, skeletal, broken. Directly underneath was a burlap bag, half open, filled with bones. We went straight to the police station and handed it in."

"It couldn't be David, too soon if that's what you are thinking," Griffith said. "Bodies take a year to decompose underground, less so in the open air and cold weather, still too soon." A clinical explanation, delivered gently. He spoke in a near whisper, brought his chair closer to Barbara, their knees nearly touching.

Mel had leaned back in his chair and almost tipped backwards, the patterned carpet scrunched under his legs. He righted himself and said, "What are your instructions?"

"What do you mean instructions?" Griffith asked.

He sounded steely, unmoved by a distraught father's distorted thinking. With his reply, Charlie had made it clear that he was in charge. The question would not be answered.

I was keeping track of all that was said, all that was unsaid, gestures and body language and Charlie's skill at modulating his tone when necessary, his calmness. The room went dark and something rattled in the kitchen.

"My sister's down from Boston," Barbara said.

Then, with effort, she pulled herself out of her chair and went around the room turning on lights.

"I'm scared of nightfall," she said, shuffling back into her chair with a moan.

There was no Christmas tree up in the house, no decorations on the front lawn, no moon. This was a house darkened by misery. Even if David was found alive, his parents would never get over the experience of sudden, intense grief.

"Charlie's right," Peg said. "It's too soon for those bones to be David's."

"He's <u>someone'</u>s son," Barbara continued. "His loved ones are somewhere wondering what happened to him."

Griffith said, "We don't know if the bones are male or female right now."

"I'm thinking of <u>my </u>son," Barbara said.

Mel reached out for her arm but she withdrew it. How quickly one becomes aware of disruption in a relationship when it isn't ones' own. I had learned during my course that couples often split after the death of a child. It was not our job to comment on such after- effects of tragedy, but relatives of victims had to be reminded often of procedure and Charlie was now in charge; the Rizzos had to digest that and renounce unilateral action.

The silence in the room was deeper now, the exterior darkness refracted through the windows in its soft artificial light, the branches of trees alive in silhouette on the kitchen walls. As we said our good-byes and stepped onto the driveway, the cold air demanded attention and we all stopped talking. It was Christmas but it made no difference, Barbara said, the exact words I had recently said to myself. Then Mel lead her back into the house and we were alone, the three of us—Charlie, Peg and I—leaning against Charlie's car.

"We'll have to continue working, Peg," Charlie said. "Have you got get-away plans?"

"No, I'll be around. I never leave in the middle of an investigation anyway," she said.

"Me neither," said Charlie.

"He may have been killed," Peg said without emotion. Out of range of the despondent parents, we could speak freely to one another.

"Or kidnapped," I offered tentatively.

"Or kidnapped," Charlie said.

We had not been formally introduced. He shook my hand and held my eyes for a beat. I said my goodbyes and left them there in their private conversation but as soon as I was on the road, I didn't want to be alone. The long road back to my parents' house loomed. It had started to snow, big wet flakes that melted as soon as they hit the windshield. I was restless and couldn't remember the last time I'd had sex. Sergeant De Beyer's eyes and Charlie Griffith's handshake had stirred me. I called my soldier friend, Rosie, who agreed to meet me at Jane's Place in Redhook. Her voice through the Bluetooth was comical. She was training to be a standup, the absurdity of war her primary subject.

There are some people we meet without having known they existed for most of our lives and it is as though we have been friends forever. This is the way it was with me and Rosie. We had met in boot camp and, when I returned to my hometown, she followed. Having very little family and nowhere else to go, there would be at least one person she knew, she had said. She got a certificate as a personal trainer and took a job at a gym in Rhinebeck where I worked out.

I arrived at Jane's first, sat on a bar stool and waited. I wasn't in a talkative mood and I didn't want to drink. I just sat there, glancing up at the TV now and again, all holiday joy and celebration. The bartender left me alone and so did the other customers. They were mostly in pairs anyway. I went over to the juke box to select a tune. Sergeant De Beyer slid next to me. I could feel his heat.

"Can I buy you a drink?" he asked.

"Sure," I said.

His voice was deep and relaxed. It was coincidence, nothing more, that we were in the same place on Christmas Eve, but then again, it wasn't. Our towns are small and there aren't many places to go at night other than bars. Jane's is a restaurant bar, and it has a juke box. Strangers dance, strangers hook up. I had never seen Ed there before.

He stared down into his glass and drained it. It looked like wheat beer.

"I'll have the same," I said, not really wanting to drink, but not wanting to be impolite either.

He ordered my beer and we walked back over to the juke box. Rosie had arrived, taken a booth, and waved.

"You'll have to excuse me, Ed. My friend has arrived. I promised her a heart to heart. Thanks for the drink. I owe you one. You got me out of my mood."

"Dance first?" Ed said, and smiled.

I signaled to Rosie and she gave me the thumbs up. "I can't remember the song," I told her later. "He held me close. I didn't mind."

CHAPTER 3

Peg had asked me often if I thought it was a good idea for me to be on a case involving a veteran and I'd said yes immediately, yes it's a good idea, how could it not be a good idea? But then I had moments, hours and days when I wasn't so sure. I never reported my doubts to Peg because she would have asked me to recuse myself, I'm sure of it. It would have been too difficult to explain, before I myself understood it, how I used my war readiness to take me down tunnels like second sight. I was already inside David's soldier head: what he would do, and wouldn't do. And Christa's mother was as familiar to me as David, though I didn't know how familiar until much later. Where had I seen her before? If she had been a beggar in a war zone with a palatial home in the Caribbean, I would not have been surprised. And if I'd met her in Iraq, hands-down, I would have reported her to the United States Army Criminal Investigations Command and watched happily as they reeled her in. What evidence did I have that Mrs. Woolf was like one of the vultures operating for their own gain in the battlefield? None, so far. Or, rather, she scared me into fight response, my armored gear snapped solid around me. I wanted to pull my gun as soon as I set foot in the sterile trailer she called home. I didn't know we were just dipping that day and there was more to come.

Peg had her own fears—who doesn't—and on our way to visit Mrs. Woolf for the first time she told me about one of them: she didn't enjoy visits to trailer parks. It wasn't snobbishness, she explained, no, none of that. "I could have easily ended up in one myself after my husband left," she said. And she went on with her thesis: A trailer is not a house, a trailer park is not a park and a trailer development is not developed, it is underdeveloped. Not fifty yards from the trailer park where Mrs. Woolf lived, on the west side of Rte. 9, was the Franklin Delano Roosevelt estate. A verdant landscape, a mansion, a barn, a garden, a library with leather-bound books, a view of the river, photographs of privileged children in pinafores with nursemaids and nannies. These contrasts of class, old money and new, poverty and wealth, are commonplace in upstate New York.

We turned left into the parking lot, the estate behind us, and within a minute were walking through a dense wood, ankle-deep in leaves covered with snow and ice. The trailers were zoned, another euphemism. In the outside world, zoning is a marketable commodity but like all else here—the postage stamp gardens, the exposed overhead wiring—it was a euphemism, totally false. As was Mrs. Woolf. First question: Why hadn't we called ahead to make an appointment?

"Your daughter's boyfriend is missing," Peg said.

"The police have been here."

"And now we are here. May we come in?"

A slight grimace lowered the corners of Mrs. Woolf's fussily lined lips. She was a well-dressed, small-boned woman of fifty or so with dyed black, coiffed hair in a retro-style that was made popular in the 1960's by Jackie Kennedy. She'd come down in life, that was clear, and her effort to maintain dignity amidst poverty might have been seen by some as heroic. But she didn't fool me and she didn't fool Peg, both of us aware that we were on to something big here. I could see it in Peg's eyes and her eager expression. Why hadn't Charlie Griffith told us about Mrs. Woolf?

"Please sit down," she said pointing to the love seat on the other side of a glass coffee table. There was nothing on it: no books, no knickknacks, no flowers, no bowls of fruit. It had been polished to a sparkle.

Her voice had a trace of a foreign accent, one I'd heard before but couldn't place right away. I opened my notebook and looked around. If Christa had ever lived here, there was no sign of her. The mementos of youth that most parents save— posters, drawings, stuffed animal mascots, framed photos and photo albums—were absent. In their place were replica Rodin sculptures and Impressionist prints, leather furniture unscarred by a child's antics, and a Burmese cat that matched the tasteful décor. She rubbed against my leg and purred.

"I didn't know Christa still had a boyfriend," Mrs. Woolf said.

"Christa didn't tell you she was living with David Rizzo?" Peg said.

"No."

"Has Christa been here Mrs. Woolf?" I asked.

"I give her money, food. She is not permitted to stay in this house unless she's clean."

"Clean?"

"Not using drugs. A time comes when we have to give up on things, Ms. Singer, stop trying. What's the good? Nothing can get my daughter off drugs."

"How do you know?" I asked

"Know what?"

"That Christa won't ever get off drugs?"

She got up from the couch and pulled her skirt to her knees, offered us some tea.

"Something herbal," Peg said. "Peppermint if you have it."

"I'll do the same," I said as she moved unsteadily into the kitchen, her hands trembling as she poured out the water into three mugs and placed them on a small tray.

"And where did Christa go when she left here?" I asked.

"I don't know. She only stayed for an hour day before yesterday."

"And Christa's father, where is he?" I asked.

"He's traveling. Japan I think."

"Are you divorced? Separated?" Peg asked.

"We never got divorced."

"I see," Peg said, a neutral tone. She paused and wrote some notes. Mrs. Woolf cleared her throat. "She was a bad girl, a very bad girl. Everyone in town knew it," she continued, her voice shallow and hoarse. "Christa threw big parties whenever we were away. I didn't always live in a trailer, Ms. Singer, let me assure you."

"We'd like to talk to her," Peg said.

"I hope you find her. Truly, I hope you do."

"Where shall we begin looking?" I asked.

"Her father might know. That's what I told the police."

"But he is traveling, you say," Peg said.

"Yes. But he might know. They are close."

Peg continued, "Is there anything else you can tell me that might be helpful? Both David and Christa seem to have disappeared yet you didn't report her missing."

"I'd have to say it doesn't concern me, Ms. Singer. I wish you all the best in your investigation."

Peg put her mug down on the glass-topped table. It made a slight squeak, ceramic on glass, which gave me goose bumps. Or perhaps it was Mrs. Woolf's formality, as jarring in the trailer park setting as her lack of concern for her daughter.

"We'll leave you now Mrs. Woolf. Please call if you think of anything at all and we'll let you know how we're doing from time to time," Peg said, handing her a card.

"I'd appreciate that," Mrs. Woolf said, politely.

"No problem," Peg said. And then she began a chit-chat about the FDR estate, its beauty and historical significance, but Mrs. Woolf was eager to say good-bye.

* * *

"I want very much to see you," I wrote Sergeant De Beyer in an email. I stored it in draft mode and went back to surfing a dating site. It was 4 a.m. and the demons of the night had settled in. I had to move out of my parents' place. As I was finally earning money, it would happen soon. I asked everyone I knew to keep their eye out for reasonable rental, east or west of the river, I didn't care what town as long as it was in Ulster or Dutchess County. The thought, of moving, of moving on, of a boyfriend, of establishing my reputation as a PI, were the only comforts in the tense darkness. I got off the dating site and typed up my notes: the interview with Mrs. Woolf, the facts of the case so far, holes in the story, many of them. As soon as it was light, I showered and dressed. A list of unanswered questions lay exposed in my notebook on the table. I read them over, then folded the moleskin into my backpack with a waxed paper bag of cut apple, celery and carrots to sustain me until lunch time. The Rizzos had requested another visit.

As soon as I was in the car, I realized how fatigued I was. I drove cautiously, keeping to the speed limit. Even the main roads had patches of black ice and I had to stay alert. The Rizzo's driveway was an ice rink. I flipped the car around, not entirely intentionally, and faced it sideways. I'd already seen evidence— occasional harsh words—of this once happy couple disintegrating since the disappearance of their son. Their driveway hadn't been sanded or salted so I got out of the car and looked for a barrel, but there was none. No barrel, and no noise from inside the house. I returned to my car and waited for Peg to arrive, kept the motor running, turned on the radio, turned it off. A bird flapped down onto a nearby tree, probably a turkey vulture or a hawk. Then someone called out and I reluctantly got out of the car and walked along the gravel driveway to a side entrance where Barbara was holding the door ajar. It didn't seem sensible to ignore her even though I assumed, wrongly as it turned out, that Peg would not want me talking to her on my own.

"Do you carry a gun?" Barbara asked as soon as I took off my boots and jacket in the mud room. She spoke quietly.

"I have one. But if we need back-up, we call in the police. We don't take unnecessary risks."

I regretted the half-lie. For whose benefit was I lying? Peg took risks all the time and I knew I would, too, soon enough. Hadn't I been a soldier? Isn't risk axiomatic on the battlefield? Still, I didn't like the question. The gun was mostly for my own protection. Right now it was tucked into a holster in the small of my back under my fleece.

My cell phone rang, Peg to say she was in New Paltz and we should meet up at her office at noon. I had given up the idea that I'd be working with her together all the time but was I ready, really ready, to be on my own? So much bravado when I had first met Peg. I can do it, I've been a soldier, I had told her. And then all the self-doubts surfacing. Peg obviously thought I knew what to do, or would learn what to do as I worked. If there is no trust between partners, where are we, she always said. With this phone call, she had given me permission to initiate a line of questioning, or research, without her permission.

"What's going on?" I asked Barbara.

"I'm worried ," she said. "I think we're being followed."

"How do you know?"

"Strange noises at night, flashlights. I'm scared. Mel didn't want me to say anything. Please don't tell him I said anything."

She was out of control, sinking. A bird flapped away into the early morning light near the window but I still couldn't make out what it was.

"Let's call the police, ask Charlie Griffith to come back," I said.

"No. Can you stay here? Do you carry a gun?"

"I can't protect you, Barbara. You didn't hire us to protect you. We'll have to call the police."

I sent Barbara inside and stayed in the mudroom to make the call. Peg didn't like it when a client with-held information or took over the investigation. Stress induced client vigilantes, she called them. It wasn't always fair or kind but that's what she thought at times. "PIs are not hired guns," she said. Then she put Charlie Griffith on the phone.

"Why didn't she tell me when I was there?" he asked

"She's scared, not thinking clearly," I said.

"And her husband?"

"I can't answer that right now. It is an important question though. Barbara spoke to me in the mudroom. She asked me not to say anything to Mel."

Gloomy day, clouds darkening the sky, the back yard thick as night, a long night not yet over. I peered into the distant shadows, the tracing of a quarter moon, otherwise nothing. Whoever or whatever was lurking was no longer there or had never been there. The overcast day was a canvas, Barbara's fear and sorrow projected onto the dappled mid-winter landscape of snow-covered pines, stiff spindly oaks and white birches.

I went into the kitchen where both Barbara and Mel were sitting at the table drinking cups of coffee.

"I'll stay until the officer arrives," I said. "Tell him everything. Don't hold back any information. Please keep in mind that though we work privately, it's always in collaboration with law enforcement. Whatever you say to me I eventually share with others as long as the investigation is ongoing. It's not like the confidentiality you have with a lawyer or a doctor, Barbara. And you and Mel have to be working together on this, no secrets between you or unilateral action."

If Mel had heard the conversation I'd just had with Barbara in the mud room, he didn't let on. " Do you agree with Barbara that someone is following you, Mel?"

"Yes," he said.

"And why didn't you say something before?"

"I don't want them to know we are talking to the police."

"Who's them?"

"I don't know."

"Have you had a ransom note? Has David been kidnapped?" I asked.

"No. But they are there. The police might scare them away. Maybe they've come to tell us something about our son. Maybe it is our son," Barbara said.

"Let's see what the police have to say about this," I said.

"It's good of you to have come so early in the morning," Mel said.

"It is my duty to come when I am called," I said, a soldier's words. I hadn't yet made the transition to civilian life. I could have said, "It's my job," but I didn't.

"Do you mind if we watch some TV while we wait? It takes my mind off things," Barbara said. She picked up the remote and flicked on a small TV on the counter. I helped Mel clear the table and stack the dishwasher. We worked slowly without talking. There is always solace in domestic tasks.

The news was tough that day. A young woman soldier, a nurse, six months pregnant, had been killed at Fort Bragg by a colleague in the intelligence unit, an accomplished guy who spoke Farsi and Arabic. Three tours as a translator in Iraq, home on leave, and he went berserk. The woman's husband, a Captain, was still overseas and she'd flown back home to give birth to their baby. What did I think of this horrible event Barbara wanted to know?

"I am not an expert," I said. "Why don't we change the channel?"

So we watched Good Morning America and learned how to cook a weight reduction vegetable casserole.

* * *

"Whoever is prowling round here is long gone by now," Sergeant De Beyer said after he had searched the grounds.

"That's what I'm worried about," Mel said. "That you've chased them away. Please don't put on any patrols, okay? We'll manage."

"We'll patrol in an unmarked car, how's that?"

"Better," Mel said. "I keep hoping our son is trying to contact us."

It was an abrupt parting without extended goodbyes. I escaped into my car and turned on the radio to a local country station, or maybe it was a local Christian country station, I could never tell for a while. The smooth wall of safety in the Rizzo home had vanished and there were cracks everywhere.

CHAPTER 4

Two days later, Barbara called the office to tell us they had hired a psychic. On one level, this was a shock as Mel and Barbara both gave the impression of having been well grounded until their son disappeared. On another, it was no surprise at all. What had we accomplished so far? Not very much. Desperate and scared and sad, Peg reminded me. What if her beloved daughter had disappeared? She wouldn't be able to account for her actions or state of mind. "Charlie was tough on them about the bag of bones but I understood why they were searching," she said.

I asked her how she knew so much about people who were virtual strangers. "Oh," she said, "I've got a few years on you, Alison."

Peg knew the psychic they had hired—her stage name was Anna Belle. She had encountered her a couple of years before on a case at the Dutchess County Fair when a man who worked the roller coaster was accused of raping a twelve-year-old local girl. The girl's father had shot him, but he'd gotten away. Anna Belle was there at the scene. She was the rapist's sometime lover. Whenever the fair came to town, they were together and she worked the Tarot cards. Off season, she lived in Kingston, and he lived in Syracuse. She told the police the girl's father had shot her man and she would have done the same, her man was a low-life, a rapist, it wasn't the first time and though she knew it, she'd hooked up with him. And she could find him, this rapist, this low-life, she had powers. The police laughed, but then took her more seriously when she came up with solid leads, nothing she might have figured out by knowing him. Peg had read about similar cases that left her wondering if there was anything to it.

"It's always best to keep an open mind," Peg said, in conclusion. "I'll let you follow up on this, Alison. It will do you good. I can see the skepticism on that smooth-skinned face of yours."

* * *

It was nearly noon when I arrived at Olana, a mansion house once owned by the Hudson River painter, Frederick Church, now a New York State Historic Site. The mansion was closed until the New Year and the 25,000 acres of serene landscape that was once Church's farm seemed the perfect place to hide a body. The vista of the river and the mountains had inspired many artists and was incredibly beautiful even on a sharply cold day with the sun peek-a-booing behind fast moving clouds. Anna Belle arrived in her ramshackle car, an old Ford Taurus rusting out on all sides. I doubted it had passed inspection. Mel and Barbara followed soon after and we set out through the snowy grounds towards the river, the psychic walking ahead with a dowsing rod. She wasn't headed for the river, she said. After speaking with Barbara and Mel in person, she felt another aura; she was searching for an unmapped underground stream surrounded by junipers. Was David buried there or captive there? Barbara asked. "Captive," Anna Belle assured her. That sounded like nonsense to me, but I said nothing. We walked down an incline where we found an old well. Any water there would have been iced over unless axed to draw from below the water line. Ana Belle stopped. "Here it is," she said. I looked around: the well was surrounded by junipers. Well, there are lots of junipers around here, I thought.

"We'll forget all this in time," Mel said mysteriously. I recalled a book by a Japanese writer in which a well is a central character and there is a person living at the bottom of the well. I imagined David's cherubic face peering up at us, the captive at the bottom of the well. The image was so vivid I could have drawn it.

We lingered at the well a long time as Anna Belle bent over the opening and recited an unintelligible incantation. She stood on one side and we stood on the other, our heads bent in a kind of prayer. I always took Peg's advice to heart, but even if I hadn't my skepticism might have softened that day. It was one of those bad days when gloom stalked me so I didn't resist relief in ceremony, however ridiculous it seemed. I bent my head and said my own silent prayer, closer to a Buddhist *metta: May we find David Rizzo alive so we won't have to confront his killers.*

"What do you see?" Barbara asked.

"A trail of tears," Anna Belle replied.

"And where will it lead?" Mel asked.

"The dead are never forgotten," Ana Belle said.

"So he's dead?" Barbara asked, her voice a riptide, rising and falling with emotion.

"No, not dead. Not yet," Anna Belle said.

She was in a trance, swaying, her head thrown back against the fallen hood of her white parka. Who wears a white parka except a child? It was then I noticed her tanned face, her wrinkles, the scar under her left ear, her thin blond hair, an old crone. She might have been Native, indigenous, a shaman. And then she stopped chanting and we stopped whatever it was we were doing. Anna Belle's sentence echoed: *The dead are never forgotten.*

We walked back up the long incline to the parking lot, the ice-crusted snow churned to powder as we followed the path we'd made going down. Barbara asked, "Are we lost?" though the mansion loomed in front of us and our three cars were already in view.

There was nothing to report to Peg when I returned to the office except for the psychic's assertion that David was not dead yet. "Meaning what?" Peg asked.

"I suppose it means that he is still alive," I said.

"But that he won't be alive for long," Peg said.

"Are we to believe this prophecy?" I asked.

"We are to believe nothing, we are to believe everything," Peg said.

I had a bad feeling again as I had the day in Mrs. Woolf's trailer that we were on to something bigger than a disappearance and that David was mixed up in it.

Peg noted my sour expression and asked me to stay for supper, but I needed to get away to break the melancholy that had fallen on me at the well. I knew it was unprofessional to leave the office without debriefing and planning our next moves, so I said I wanted to return to Mrs. Woolf's trailer and case it. Peg didn't object, or perhaps she hadn't heard me. I spent the rest of the day bivouacked behind a tree in the trailer park.

Mrs. Woolf returned around 8 p.m. carrying two sacks marked "Culinary Institute" where she had said she worked as a part-time secretary. I would have to go up there and ask some questions about her, perhaps tomorrow. The hours behind the tree yielded nothing except the observation that Christa's mother returned home late from work and that she looked fit as she lifted the heavy bags into the trailer.

"What we'll need, eventually, is a search warrant," Peg said when I called her. She'd let me go because of my peculiar mood, she said. "You have to conserve your energy, manage your time," she said. "If there is something to be found at the trailer, we'll find it, but there's no lead except for your intuition and usually we don't stake out anything without Charlie Griffith's permission . Go home and get some rest."

So I drove home, my parents' home. The roads were empty, the bare windswept trees sentinels in the too swift passage of time. In the distance, the ever-present mountains provided constancy and embrace. The moon was full, the sky spilling with stars. I sat at the kitchen table overlooking the back woods. A snowy owl sat on the roof of the barn across the road. It had been living there for many weeks. Climate change has forced them south in search of food. Birds of prey can be agitated, but owls are serene, predators with few fears. I picked up my binoculars. My desire to see every detail of this beautiful bird and to keep looking was overwhelming. I wanted to touch its wings, stroke its head. It didn't seem real. More than once, I had tried to capture its ethereal quality in tempera, in watercolor, and in oil, but had never succeeded. I turned to the note from my parents—they'd gone to see a movie— and the newspaper they'd left on the table. David Rizzo's picture was on the front page, the word MISSING across the top. I took out my sketchbook and drew his face at the bottom of a well and then I went to bed and fell into a dreamless sleep until morning.

CHAPTER 5

D avid and Christa had last been seen on the footpath near The Eagle and the police had interviewed the bartender and the regulars, but not returned. Peg asked me to go back; she was sure a piece of the story was missing. It was New Year's Eve day, the 31st of December, and Peg had plans that night to meet-up with her daughter and her new boyfriend at Jane's for a late-night cabaret. Rosie and I planned to be there also. All being well, I'd have plenty of time to get home, rest, shower, and join them by 9 p.m.

The Eagle was a saloon with ramshackle tables scattered around in no discernible practical or aesthetic pattern. The floor was covered with sawdust, a quaint touch. The only wall decorations were beer advertisements, some of them old and stained with cigarette smoke. The place smelled bad. It was about 2 p.m. when I walked in, dark outside, another storm blowing in over the mountains. There were a couple of guys at the far end of the bar watching the news on TV, otherwise the place was empty.

"You'd never know it was New Year's Eve," I said as I sat down. I'd been a shy kid, sidelined by my brothers' banter, but the shyness had vanished in the military where I had learned to speak up and speak loud in the midst of turmoil on the ground, or inside a rumbling tank with loud-mouthed, dirty-mouthed swearing soldiers. We had our own rapid-fire language, none of it pretty. Now, I could sit at a bar and shoot the breeze with anyone—ordinary people, extraordinary people, high class and low. No one forgot I was a girl and I got hit on plenty—in the army, at the bars. In the past, I hadn't been a PI, I'd been a vet, and this impressed a few guys, scared off others. If they came on to me, I took what I wanted when I wanted and left the rest, honest when I needed to be, deceptive if it suited me. I'd told Peg all of it and as soon as I did she made it clear: no deception, I had to state my purpose.

"You working for the police?" the bartender asked.

"The family."

"Mind if I take a look at your ID?"

"No problem."

I opened my wallet and watched the man's eyes. He was sober.

"Christa was a regular," he said eagerly. Either he enjoyed being interviewed—it broke the boredom of his work—or he was a good guy with a lousy job.

"The guy who was with her, David Rizzo, the guy who disappeared," he continued. "I'd never seen him before. She introduced me and they went to sit at a table in the back. Wanted to be alone I guess."

His sentences were truncated, his speech idiosyncratic, w's rounded to r's. I couldn't understand him all the time. His thick greasy hair covered a small indentation in his skull just above his ear. He had three piercings at the top and a tattoo of a soaring eagle running off the ear down the left side of his neck.

"You the owner?"

"John Burrows," and he extended his hand.

I made a note to talk to Peg about using him as an informant. He had been forthcoming right away.

"Have you been to the Ashokan Reservoir?" I asked him.

"When I was a kid. We used to fish off the banks."

"Not recently?"

"No."

"You should get up there. The eagles are back. Maybe the one on your neck will abandon you and find his mate."

He laughed and poured me a tall glass of cold water.

"I assume you're not drinking."

"Not when I'm working. So what about that afternoon?" I continued.

"It was a pretty mellow day. Christa and her guy, David, were sitting at the back sipping on some beers. She ordered a whisky chaser and another beer, but he stuck to the one. Then a couple of tough looking guys in camouflage suits came in, pulled David up by his arms, and took him outside. We all went quiet. Christa started screaming and followed them out. They shoved her away, hit her a couple of times, told her to get back inside and mind her own business. Then the guys took off with David in the truck sitting between them."

"What about the witness who said he saw them on the footpath?"

"Whoever said that was hallucinating."

"Did you tell the cops what you're telling me?"

"Sure. At least I think so. They were in a hurry, got a call about a pile-up on the Thruway. I like to gab and they rushed me."

"OK, let's get back to the truck. Can you be more specific? Did you see the license plate, any markings? What color was it?"

"Like your vest, bright red, a flatbed, pretty new."

"And the license? New York State plate?"

"No something else. Different colors. Couldn't make it out."

"What happened to Christa?"

"She came back in crying and asked to use the phone. I didn't listen in. And then she left in her car, a beat-up old Honda, blue, I think. She was wasted, I don't know how she drove. I tried to stop her but she brushed me off. You can't talk sense to an addict. Should I have called the cops? Maybe, but only in retrospect. A lot of drunks leave here for the road."

"What else can you tell me?"

"A couple of guys in here were her customers."

"She was a dealer?"

"Casual. Nothing big. She'd sell off a bag or two if she had them extra."

"And you let her?"

"The cops leave us to keep our eye on things."

"Anything else you can tell me?"

"That's about it. Never saw David and Christa after that and then I heard she's in detox and he's disappeared. I feel bad about that. Nothing I could do."

"Christa's in detox?"

"Yeah, over in Kerhonkson, Veritas Villa, good place. You didn't know?"

That took me my surprise. Veritas Villa rehab was private and someone would have had to pay for it.

I pushed back the bar chair and said, "Thanks, John. What do I owe you for the water?"

"It's on me."

Our conversation had let loose some ideas about the racket David might be involved in. If he wasn't dead and he wasn't innocent, his parents were in for a reckoning about their son.

I drew an eagle in my moleskin, underlined a few key words, and called Veritas Villa. Long story short: Christa wasn't there, had never been there, and they'd never even received a phone call inquiring about their program. So, she was still at large, hiding out somewhere. And we had to find her.

* * *

Back at the office, Peg called Charlie Griffith and put him on speaker phone.

"Did you know about the flatbed," she asked him.

"Yes, we did."

"Wish you'd told us, Charlie. Any way we can coordinate better?"

"Apologies Peg. I've been distracted, my son has been deployed to Afghanistan, third tour, other family problems at the moment. I haven't been on point."

"Sorry, Charlie."

"Glad you called Peg. Would you be able to follow a lead? An informant gave us an exact address: a log cabin on a small iced-over stream in Palenville near the swimming hole. It's Greene County so you'll be going out of your way a bit."

"So much for a nap before New Year's Eve," Peg said.

"If you get up there soon you should make it back down in plenty of time. Hot date?"

"You still married, Charlie?"

"On and off."

"OK, let's leave that one alone."

"Take care, Peg."

"Alison will be with me. No worries, Charlie. Right, Alison? You'll protect me?"

"You bet," I said, and meant it.

* * *

The red truck—no plates, no markings—was in the driveway. Smoke was coming out of the chimney and there was a car covered with a tarp in the barn. Peg backed down until we were nearly at the bottom and swung over into getaway position. Then she turned off the engine and hung a left. She called Griffith on the two-way radio, cells not working, no towers nearby. Charlie ordered us to sit tight, he'd call central dispatch to send over troopers. Smoke was coming out of the chimney, someone was warm inside the house.

But was David with them? I felt a battlefield adrenalin rush, gun at the ready. But we weren't wearing flak jackets and our guns were small caliber, tucked into holsters.

"I'm not crazy about this set-up," I said to Peg, the timbre of my voice slipping into high register. There are always so many things we don't know about ourselves. I was scared. Though we were out on the road below the cabin anyone looking out the window could spot us there in the same vulnerable position as a tank driving through a valley, mountains on both sides, undefended terrain. I had thought I was over this.

"Take it easy. This isn't a war zone," Peg said.

Our roles had switched yet again; she was protecting me. I hadn't said anything yet she knew I was edgy. Objectively, my observation made sense so I forgave myself the slip, if feeling edgy is a slip. John Burrows had said the guys who took David were wearing camouflage. Wasn't my soldier head one of the reasons Peg had agreed to my working on the case? "Undefended terrain," I said, my nerves settling as I reiterated what my brain map was telling me.

"Just remember why we are here," Peg said as the troopers pulled in front of us. "We're here for the family, to find their son, dead or alive. It's a small job compared to many others. Don't lose your focus."

"What are we looking for?" one of the troopers asked.

Peg explained: "Not sure but the red truck in the driveway is connected to the disappearance of David Rizzo down in Rhinebeck. We're the PIs hired by the family. We're working with Charlie Griffith."

"We'll go have a look and call for more back-up if we need it. Stay put. We'll let you know what's going on."

We got out of the car and followed them up the driveway until we could see the front door. It opened a crack at the first knock.

"State Police," one of the troopers said. "Would you please step outside, Miss."

The woman was young. And she looked just like her mother.

"It's Christa," I said to Peg.

"Is there anyone else in the cabin, Miss?"

"Just me," the young woman said. She was in a green night-dress patterned with over-sized neon colored flowers, her feet bare.

In war, I had learned to fear the rage of the defeated. Once released from their subservience, a kind of captivity, they become savage. And the energy of those in the grip of addiction is a similar savage energy. As the troopers threw open the door of the cabin and rushed inside, guns drawn, Christa bolted and ran down the hill into the woods not far from where Peg and I were standing. We gave chase until we could no longer see the road or the cabin. Running in bare feet without any protective clothing, Christa had covered about a mile before tripping on an an exposed root. Like a wounded dog, she crawled behind a layered glacial rock and rolled onto her side as we approached. Peg went down onto her knees next to Christa's limp, frail body, and gently rubbed her arm. "It's okay, dear, you're safe now," she said. Then she took off her jacket and put it over Christa's shoulders. I tore off my outer shirt, split it in half, and wrapped it around her feet. We held her upright between us and led her back to the cabin. She would be pulled in for questioning about David's disappearance, maybe even her drug dealing. "Where's David?" was the first thing Christa said. She didn't know who we were or where she was or what day it was but David was there, in her mind, still with her, a long lost love, someone she had grown up with and counted on.

"What are you using?" Peg asked.

"Nothing," she said.

"We'll get you to the hospital," Peg said. And then when we were back at the cabin, she asked the troopers to call an ambulance. No way to get anything sensible out of Christa Woolf until she was off the drugs. Even if it was just for a day or two, she might be able to tell us something.

The troopers—Sam and Pete—opened the truck door with a Ford master key. Nothing much inside at first glance except burlap bags and a box of used single-edged razors, every one of them soiled with dried blood.

"I think we've got a match with a bag we found down in Rhinebeck. It was filled with bones," Peg said to me and to the troopers. It didn't take much imagination to figure out what the blades were for: Someone had forgotten to toss them after stripping the bones in the burlap bag of all remaining flesh.

The car under the tarp, a blue Honda Civic, was registered to Mrs. Woolf. The battery was on a shelf. Whoever had stored it knew that Christa wouldn't have the wherewithal to put it back together. Maybe they were hoping she'd run out of food and starve to death in the house as she was almost completely broken down by malnutrition, her body eating itself. We sat her on a soft chair and covered her with blankets, fed her water, and a half-rotted apple from the bottom of the filthy refrigerator. She had probably been in the cabin on her own for weeks, since the day David had been hauled out of The Eagle, possibly, or soon thereafter, barely existing, in and out of chemical dreams, dosed up by whoever had brought her here, a stockpile of syringes on the middle shelf of the fridge, Christa's meal of choice.

"This your place?" Peg asked.

"No," Christa said. "Not my place. Funny huh?"

"Nothing's too funny right now," Peg said. "Who belongs to the truck?"

"A couple of David's army buddies."

During the forty or so minutes it took for the ambulance to arrive, we searched the grounds and the garbage overflowing onto the back patio: empty bags of chips, empty tin cans, moldy tea bags, decaying corn cobs. It looked like a bear or raccoon had helped itself to a hearty meal or two while the person inside was starving.

"I don't think David was here," Peg said as we drove away. "The two army buddies separated them, brought her here, parked the vehicles. But they were foolish to leave the bags. They can be traced. Did you catch the logo? A farm on Rte. 28."

For some reason I felt like laughing. What was bubbling up was the certainty that a bone-filled burlap bag was another of David's signatures or markings. He was leaving tracks, like a bear leaves its spoor: his drawings, the bones, Christa herself. But with all his skills, all his intelligence, he hadn't been able to save her from the sequester in the cabin. Or he might have deliberately left her there, hoping to keep her safe. There was no way to be sure.

CHAPTER 6

Mrs. Woolf had told the human resources department at the Culinary Institute in Hyde Park that she had a green card but it took her a while to produce it. They had a photocopy in their files and they let me look at it. A photograph, a fingerprint, a name, date of birth, a string of numbers, and the words "Permanent Residence Card" across the top. I knew a half-dozen Iraqis who could have forged it. But why would Mrs. Woolf have had to forge a green card if she was married to an American and had been in the United States so many years?

"Did you do a background check?" I asked Shay Brown, the Human Resources officer.

"No, the card was enough," he said. "Mrs. Woolf lives locally and she's been in the U.S. for a while, raised her kid here, so we figured for part-time work—fifteen hours a week—it wasn't necessary."

We were sitting in his office overlooking the quadrangle at the center of the building, a former Jesuit monastery sitting on a hill overlooking the Hudson.

"Where is she from originally?" I asked.

I still hadn't placed the accent though I should have. There were Iranians in Iraq, many of them, and they all spoke Farsi, not Arabic.

"Iran," Shay said. "But she says she's Persian. Upper class, refined. We were happy to have her here, an elegance about her that suits our mission—internationalism in cuisine. We turn out premier chefs who find positions all over the world."

When he escorted me out we had to pass through the campus grounds, students in their white smocks and toque hats rushing from one class to another, chatting incessantly, like students everywhere.

"Does Mrs. Woolf have friends here?" I asked.

"She keeps to herself, I think, but sometimes she eats in one of the restaurants at the end of her working day and the permanent staff know her. I never saw her with anyone at a table."

"A loner," I said.

"I was always interested in finding out more about her, but she seemed shy and I didn't push it. In the five years she's been here I'd say we have only talked two or three times at any length and it was usually about her work. She's a pool secretary—efficient, amenable—and works for anyone who needs her."

We were nearly at the parking lot when I spotted Mrs. Woolf sitting on a bench with a steaming paper cup. Her shift was about to begin. I'd been delayed and had been hoping to miss her. I didn't greet her, just headed for my car. I interpreted her expression as dumb fear, like an animal caught in the headlights, but it could have just as easily been defiance. Her face was a mask and she sat absolutely still inside her long, down coat, her head hatless, her hair as perfectly coiffed as the day we had interviewed her in the trailer. A wind wafted up, but she kept on sitting there, sipping on her cup, until I turned on my engine and drove away. I felt as though our wordless encounter had been a stand-off and that she had gotten the better of me, that I would find nothing incriminating about her, and that she knew it. More importantly, I wasn't satisfied with the information about Mrs. Woolf—first name Farideh—the human resources officer had offered. But what else had I been expecting to hear?

* * *

Mrs. Woolf returned home at 9 p.m. that night. I was waiting for her behind the tree and as she put her key in the lock, I stepped onto the gravel path and said, "Good Evening, Mrs. Woolf, I'd like to ask you a few more questions." My voice was firm and determined; I had gotten into an occupier's state of mind and had set up an ambush. I had no self-doubts in that moment, but I also had not planned another line of questioning. My appearance was an attempt at pressure, nothing more. I wanted Mrs. Woolf to know that I was watching her, but I was on her property; she was angry. Hadn't she cooperated enough? Told me what I wanted to know? "I don't think you have told us everything," I said. "Just get away from me," she said.

And so I left and drove into the night without even mentioning that her daughter had been found, that she'd been taken to the hospital, and released.

* * *

Peg was not pleased with me. I was still a novice, she said, and hadn't yet learned not to be dishonest in the presence of a suspect. Though I was entitled to investigate, ask questions, and move freely, I should have at least greeted Mrs. Woolf at the Culinary Institute. Instead, I had behaved furtively. And then to turn up at her trailer unexpectedly, to wait for her in ambush? This wasn't an officially sanctioned stake-out and could be construed as stalking or harassment. What kind of childish game was I playing?

I had some hard thinking to do, I told Peg. My mind was racing around every possibility, every corner. I wasn't happy with myself that I'd not been able to identify Mrs. Woolf's accent."But now you know she's Iranian, so we move on. We find out if it's relevant or not," Peg said. "Keep your focus. We're looking for David Rizzo, dead or alive. What's wrong with you, Alison? You have to stay on point." I didn't know if this was a rhetorical question or if Peg knew what was wrong with me. I was sure she did—she wasn't naive—but had decided not to bring up PTSD yet again. She'd mentioned it, so had I. She'd even said to me, with a wry affectionate twist in her voice, that I should pretend I was normal. So that's what I did most of the time.

* * *

Peg was in the car when she heard the call come in on the radio. The propane delivery man had noticed a strange smell. He thought a bear had gotten into the house and was hibernating there. He looked in the window and saw Christa. She was lying on her stomach in front of the cold wood stove. The wooden plank under her left cheek was bloody. Her legs were splayed open, her toes facing inward like a bow-legged dancer. Her ripped dress hung around her waist. The tracks on her arms were fresh, oozing next to healed scars. "Someone forced her. The expression on her face isn't addict ecstatic, it's terrified," Peg said to the first troopers who arrived. One of them put his arm around her shoulders until the shaking subsided. The scene was mythic: a woman's violated body, the detritus of war.

"Check for rape," Peg said to Charlie.

It had taken Charlie too long to arrive. She couldn't wait for him to be there, Peg told me later. He saw what she had seen immediately, a parent's nightmare, and understood. I arrived about thirty minutes later.

"It looks like soldiers. War rape," I said. "I think we should be searching for AWOL soldiers, on-leave soldiers, soldiers messed up in some kind of a scheme or deal, drugs, but not necessarily drugs, former friends of David's or maybe current friends of David's. I'm beginning to think the psychic Mel and Barbara hired is right, he's still alive. And I'm worried that Mel and Barbara know he's alive and are protecting him."

Peg walked outside. The trees were twisted, covered with frozen lichen, the dead in the dead of winter. Charlie said to me: "Will you inform Christa's mother?"

"I don't know why we didn't protect her." Peg said. "Why did we let her come back here. She was marked."

"We weren't paying attention," Charlie said.

"That's not good enough," I said.

It slipped out and I was sorry, even ashamed.

"I want Alison to inform Christa's mother," Peg said.

She was talking to me without looking at me, as though I wasn't there. "She'll know what to say. It will be an act of contrition."

This was another warning. I had to shape up if I wanted to continue working for Private Investigator Margaret Singer.

* * *

The sky went dark and the afternoon fell chill on the mountains as I drove south towards Hyde Park. Only the whirr of the tires was audible inside the car, the radio silenced.

It was a Sunday and there were a lot of children playing outside. I walked straight up the path and knocked on Mrs. Woolf's door. She stepped outside without her coat and stood as stolid as an old, veined tree.

"It's all right, dear," she said.

"Christa didn't make it, Mrs. Woolf. I'm very sorry. They released her from the hospital and she went back to the cabin."

"She was in the hospital?"

"Yes," I said.

I spoke slowly, precisely. It was the best I could do. Then I leaned forward and pulled her body into mine. But only my tears flowed.

* * *

The wind had subsided and there hadn't been any snow for a couple of days. The roads were busy again with shoppers heading for the holiday sales in Harriman and Kingston. Rosie called to say she'd found me an apartment in Redhook on top of a free-standing garage. The couple that owned the place were writers, quiet, nice people, and the rent was reasonable. No pets, no parties and I'd be near Jane's. I put my money down and moved in the next day. Packing up my belongings, I was aware of the emptiness my parents would feel when I was gone, but my mother assured me it couldn't be worse than the months I'd been in Iraq and Afghanistan. I'd still be close enough to come home for Sunday dinners, holidays, or whenever I felt like it, she said. My dad said nothing, my brothers said nothing, they just helped me load my belongings into the car.

It wasn't like walking away into war so why make a drama? It wasn't a drama.

* * *

Once upon a time, a man at a pool hall said to me, "You're unlucky in small things." He was referring to the bad shot I'd made but I took his commentary as a jinx. My boyfriend at the time was indifferent to my moods and critical of me in most respects. He walked away and went to the bar where he could drink but I still couldn't. I put my pool cue down and any advantage I might have had in the game through skill and perseverance was lost, my confidence shattered. Then I went outside to get some air. I had assumed my star ascendant and it had fallen. I was only seventeen. I walked down to the river and stood there for a long time in the fading light. The ice was dissolving. I drew courage from the observation that nothing ever stays the same. That man, my opponent at the pool table who had pushed me off my game and triggered defeatism in my spirit, had done it deliberately because I had been winning, because I was a young woman. His words were not accidental; they were premeditated. It was my first encounter with deliberate cruelty. By the end of the episode, I'd broken up with my boyfriend. It was a turning point, I was angry, I didn't want to go to college, and I wanted to shoot my boyfriend. Where did this killing energy come from? I was a girl. Are girls allowed to have these impulses? Then I was in the army and all my fantasies about killing came true, but not for long. I discharged my gun's bullets into flesh, blood flowed, men and women died under my boots.

This strange, disturbing memory came to me as I drove across the river to meet Peg and Charlie Griffith at the trooper station in New Paltz. Charlie was fifty-two years-old, six years younger than Peg Singer, and I could not imagine that he was ever cruel. He was a burly, handsome, easy-going, community-minded, family man. He had received numerous awards and accolades, all well deserved.

"What we have to discuss today is very difficult," he began. "I hope you'll consider what I say carefully. I've told my assistant not to interrupt us unless there's an emergency."

In the corner, a filing cabin stood open, Charlie's jacket hanging on a peg with a couple of sedate scarves and hats. The office was unusually tidy for a police station and there were family photos and children's drawings on every surface, plants on the windowsill, a home away from home. I felt comfortable and ready for anything Charlie might have to say to us despite the preamble.

"The FBI has assigned an agent to the Rizzo case. She'll be working out of this office. Her name is Pat Dolan and we'll all have to defer to her. The Patriot Act has been invoked."

"Not good," Peg said.

"I agree. But we have no choice, not an ounce of choice. The law's the law. Are you with me?"

"I understand, but I don't understand," I said. "A young man, a soldier, is missing. He's a former employee of the U.S. government. His girlfriend has been murdered. Why would the FBI be interested?"

"I don't know yet. And we may never know. That's a big problem for local law enforcement. The FBI is not obliged to tell us anything."

He paused and walked to the window.

"My son has just been sent over again, Peg."

"I'm sorry, Charlie."

"I worry about him every day."

"I'm sorry, Charlie. You know that Alison is a veteran," and she turned to me.

For a moment I waited to speak. I wanted to say something hopeful, that his son would be okay, that he wouldn't be hurt, that he would return alive and eager to pick up his life again. But what was the point of telling more lies or half-lies? A third tour, no comfort possible.

"Charlie," I said. But I couldn't go on. Somewhere in another room, a woman was humming.

"She sings in a choir," Charlie said.

He was a gentleman of the old school: he had values, he was idealistic, he cared about people. Peg was a little bit in love with him, I could see that.

"So when is the agent arriving?" Peg asked.

"Soon. I'll keep you posted. In the meantime, we'll carry on with the investigation. Don't say anything to the Rizzos just yet."

* * *

The week continued, all of it bitterly cold. The bright sky dimmed and it snowed heavily, a winter wonderland. Despite the challenging weather, the psychic wanted to return to the well at Olana. I went along, if only to keep Mel and Barbara company. Over the long weeks of waiting, David's absence had become a presence, and their mood had toggled between despair, resignation and hope. When we found a burlap bag under the lip of the well's opening, their spirits lifted and so did mine. It was surrounded by small rocks piled in a cairn. Then Anna Belle's powers faltered and she had nothing more to say. I bent down to pick up the bag, rattled the bones, David's signature. "It's a message from David," I said. "He wants you to know he's still alive." I didn't open the bag to check if the bones were bloody or bare. I'd leave that to Charlie and his forensic team.

We took a last look at the landscape, commented on its eternal beauty, and got into our cars. I called Peg to meet me at the Rizzo's. I hadn't been doing the work long, but knew when clients required bolstering; now was such a time.

"Any psychic has limitations," Peg told them. "Let's stay with your instinct that David is alive and somewhere nearby. The bag at the well is a good sign."

"We were walking past the bridge the other day," Barbara said. "The graffiti on the wall has been blacked out with a thick brush."

"You should have called me immediately," Peg said. "Nothing you see, hear, or casually notice, stays with you. Pick up the phone and call me immediately."

"We didn't think it was anything," Mel said.

"Deciding if a clue is important is not your job, it's my job, Alison's job, Charlie Griffith's job. I'll call him now. Whoever blacked out the graffiti bought his supplies somewhere."

"My Home Depot credit card is gone," Barbara said. "I rarely use it but I was looking for it the other day and it's definitely gone."

"Say this mantra, Barbara: I will call Peg immediately."

"Peg's right," Mel said.

"I'll call you immediately," Barbara said.

* * *

Special Agent Pat Dolan arrived on Monday, January 21. The first thing I noticed: FBI dress code. She wore a well-cut black pant suit that set off her hazel eyes and thick shoulder length dirty-blond hair cut into an angled page-boy, bangs from the top of her crown falling neatly around her chiseled model-like features. She had broad shoulders; swimming was her sport in college we learned later. The training at the Academy had done the rest: she was buff. She took off her jacket and her shoulder holster with an easy physical self-confidence. She was probably not even thirty but spoke with the poise of an experienced agent. The friendly banter ended, the smile disappeared, and she was all business, the transformation complete. I was envious of the agent's wardrobe and clout, but not much else. Peg was envious of her youthful body. Both of us left the meeting with the distinct impression that we were under surveillance; one misstep and Agent Dolan would reel us in. Two nights later there was a knock on my door. It was 1 a.m. I picked up my gun from the bedside table, slipped on shoes and a robe, and shook myself awake. "Who is it?" I shouted.

"Agent Dolan."

I opened the door a crack, my gun in my left hand at my side.

An unmarked black car idled in the driveway, a bald-headed man at the wheel. I couldn't make out his face.

"Can I come in for a minute?"

"Do you always make courtesy calls at this time of night?" I asked sarcastically. I didn't appreciate being treated like an enemy alien.

"I was just passing by," she said disingenuously.

"At this time of night? We go to sleep early in the country."

"We didn't get to talk personally at the meeting the other day," she said.

"I get it. You want to remind me of protocol."

I sat down in my favorite reading chair and turned on the light, put the gun down next to the 800-page Trollope I was reading, "He Knew He Was Right." I wanted to get back to it. There was more wisdom in that book than in twenty Agent Dolans. Why had I ever wanted to be an agent, a job I'd considered—briefly—when I got out of the army?

"Please sit down," I said pointing to a straight-backed wooden chair.

"No I'm fine, thanks. I'll be on my way in a minute or two. Are you clear that you must turn over all evidence?"

"We always work collaboratively with law enforcement. But we represent the Rizzo family. Have you been to see Ms. Singer?"

"You are under our jurisdiction. How long did you say you'd been licensed?"

"I'm working for Peg Singer. Please direct your questions about me to her. She's been working as a private investigator for nearly thirty years and has cooperated with the FBI many times. I don't think she ever had surprise visits in the dead of night. That's something altogether new."

"Point taken. I had the impression you were something of a maverick, that you like to work on your own."

"You don't know me Agent Dolan. Let's just leave it at that for now. I won't offer you any refreshments. I have to get my beauty rest."

"I'll be on my way then. Hope to see you soon."

"Sure," I said.

Once the FBI was involved there was no guarantee about safety, I thought. Not if they could barge into someone's private space in the dead of night.

I fell asleep in the chair, the Trollope open on my lap, my gun next to the lamp on the table.

* * *

"Thank goodness for Trollope or I would never have gotten back to sleep," I told Peg at 7 a.m. over breakfast at her place.

"Sleep deprivation, interrupting our REMs, all deliberate," she said. "I think she came over here right after she left you."

"She accused me of being a maverick. I can only assume they were watching and listening to me at the trailer that night I made a fool of myself."

"They might have the trailer park wired," Peg said. "We have to turn everything over to them but they don't have to tell us anything. I'll call Charlie, get him over here. Best not to talk on the phone anymore except to make plans. It's ridiculous, but we have to throw the FBI off David's scent. He's our priority and we don't want them to find him until we do. It's impossible to know what they're pursuing here or what they'd do with him if they found him alive before we did. We have to just keep going. How about following up the bags and the bones and I'll coordinate with Charlie on this."

"I'm on it," I said.

I had internalized my soldier's salute and was standing at moral attention, poised to continue the investigation even if we had to disregard the FBI.

CHAPTER 7

After Christa's murder, after the visit to the trailer park to give her mother the somber news, after her tearless response, I came to the conclusion that Mrs. Woolf knew Christa had been endangered and had done nothing to protect her. I wanted to prove it, clearly against my orders. It wasn't enough for me that we were only working for the family, our mandate to find David Rizzo dead or alive. The image of Christa splayed on the floor, blood everywhere, arms scoured with fresh tracks, face swirling into a scream like an Eduard Munch painting, had stayed with me; I couldn't shake it. Once again, I didn't tell Peg any of this. She had asked me to pursue the burlap bags marked with a logo from a farm on Rte. 28, the bags we'd found in the red truck that day at the cabin in Palenville, and that's what I did. First, on Peg's insistence, I went to see her professor friend at Vassar College another enclave of privilege in a poor to middling town on the east side of the Hudson River just below Hyde Park. I hadn't been on a campus in a while and it felt strange. The college became co-ed in the 1960s but there are still more women than men. They all looked young to me, young and silly—if innocence is silly—as they walked across the carefully tended grounds and paths . The campus was silent, slung far enough away from the busy road to create an impression of seclusion. In some respects I envied the ivory tower; in other respects I was glad to be out of it. I'd had my adventure and, in any case, this was not a time to reminisce about my one year at Binghamton. Still, the sensation of opportunity lost remained.

I was early so I visited the art gallery, an exhibition of students' work, very inspiring. The school is strong in the arts. I took out my notebook, sketched for a few minutes and thought about David at the bottom of the well, or camped in the woods somewhere. In one image he was dead; in the other he was alive.

Professor Maggie Steed, a psychologist, had been at Vassar for twenty years. Smart and articulate, Peg had used her often as a resource and sounding board. She was responsive to phone calls within the hour and welcoming in her study. She preferred in-person interviews, if possible, she told me when we spoke on the phone. "The work is done when two people brainstorm sitting on couches," she said. "It's kinetic, ideas spark. So let's get to know each other." I told myself not to feel intimidated, but it was no use, I felt intimated. I'd read somewhere that the unconscious mind cannot be controlled. So I constructed a counter statement to steady my nerves instead: Maggie Steed is not my professor; she knows nothing of my drop-out story, or my war story. In fact, she is a paid consultant and, objectively, my employee. I shoved any self-doubts about my truncated education into the drawer where they belonged.

A tall woman, Professor Steed towered over my 5' ft. 8" frame as she held out her hand to greet me. She was wearing black jeans, a black cotton turtleneck, her feet shoeless, boots at the door, where I left mine.

"How are these bones placed in the bag?" she asked.

"Like a child's plaything," I said, though I hadn't thought of that before.

"I think whoever designed this 'toy' is more interested in the rattle of the bones than the shock one feels at opening the bag. What are the bags made of?"

"They're burlap potato bags. And they've been left open, not tied shut. They rattle as they are lifted."

"Burlap is rough and porous. Let's start there," Maggie continued. "I don't think it's an accident they were chosen as the container for the bones."

"They're very common. Every farmer uses them," I offered.

"It's more than that. If I'm not mistaken burlap was used for hair shirts in medieval times. The cloth is abrasive against the skin and if a sinner wanted to self-mortify or flagellate, he or she wore a hair shirt on Ash Wednesday."

"The soldier we are looking for is Catholic," I said. "He may know some of this history, or he may not."

"Sometimes the past is embedded in us," Maggie said. "It gets handed down in unexpected ways."

Not long ago I had been in the desert surrounded by barbed wire and Humvees. The past I'd lived, my little adventure, as I referred to it among other veterans, was already in the past. And what a strange world resides there—in the past, I thought. We live day to day and never think of the history that has brought us to a particular place, how the war in Iraq has its roots in the collapse of the Ottoman Empire in World War I, for example. Or how, before plastic, burlap was used as camouflage on soldiers' helmets. For a long time these insights reverberated: the burlap was still used in Vietnam, it was useful and, as Maggie Steed studied it, a metaphor surfaced inside the burlap bags filled with bones.

"It's obviously a projection, an emblem of how the person feels about themselves, bones without flesh, used up, rattling around, and overwhelmed with guilt and shame," Maggie continued.

"That sounds like PTSD."

"Or worse. Peg mentioned you've been in Iraq and Afghanistan. I imagine you saw a lot of that there and since you've come home."

She looked at me intently. I didn't like it. My memories of Iraq in particular—heroism, random violence, Anwar, the occupation itself, could not be reduced to symptoms. Now, in that ivory tower room, a so-called expert had reduced my deployments to PTSD. Had Peg asked Professor Maggie Steed to look me over, to make sure I wouldn't bust open, that I was reliable?

"May I call on you again?" I said as coolly as I could manage.

"Always happy to help," she said as she walked me to the door in her shoeless feet.

"It's an odd thing," I told her, "but I feel like I've known you all my life."

"I'll take that as a compliment," Maggie said.

But it wasn't a compliment. She reminded me of someone, who I couldn't say. And I was angry as hell at Peg. I held my breath as I walked down the antiseptic hallway, painted a lime green with dark wood trim. I fixated on its shabbiness and wanted to get out a paint brush to make it right.

* * *

Peg had Charlie on speaker phone as I walked into the office.

"Mel and Barbara Rizzo assume David is alive because he used Barbara's credit card at Home Depot to buy paint supplies. But it could have been someone else, the video tapes are blurry. The credit card may have been missing for a long time as Barbara doesn't go to Home Depot very often. They haven't heard from David, they haven't seen him, and they haven't heard from anyone he knew."

"Did you believe them?" Peg asked.

"Mostly I did, yes. Yes, I'd have to say," Charlie said.

"What about the Special Agent. Did she question them as well?"

"We did it together, as a team," he chuckled.

"And how did that go, Charlie?" Peg asked.

"Swimmingly."

"Are we looking for Christa's killer or David?" I asked.

"Both," Charlie said.

"Are they one and the same?"

"Hope not. What are you up to, Alison?"

"I'm following the burlap bags and the bones. I talked to a psychology professor at Vassar, helpful background. She agrees we're looking for a soldier, or soldiers. It could be David, who knows? The burlap is an emblem of self-mortification and/or an echo of the battlefield. Camouflage netting on helmets used to be made out of burlap. The person who planted the bones may be dropping clues or confessions."

"Good work, Alison. Thanks for all that. You know I'll have to pass it on to Agent Dolan."

Cries for help reverberated in my head: Christa clinging to her last minutes of life on a hardwood floor, David collecting bags of bones. Christa had been released from the hospital on her own—the judge had sent her to rehab—but she hadn't turned up there, either. And no one—no one—had protected her.

* * *

The cold was painful, it gripped the lungs. The farm on Rte. 28 was shuttered down for the winter, the owners touring the country in their RV, a neighbor said. She didn't know their name, had never bought anything from them, or bartered anything with them, and she hadn't noticed much out of the ordinary except for the woman who always wore a scarf on her head even on the hottest days. When they left for the winter, the man had come to see her just to mention they'd be away and not to be alarmed if some visitors turned up. "What visitors?" I asked.

"He said something about their son," she said.

"And has anyone turned up?"

"Not yet," she said.

"Can you describe the man?"

"About my age, early sixties, short, stout, bald, with a full beard, not handsome, rough looking, talks with an accent. Why are you looking for them?"

"Just to ask some questions about a case we're working on."

"Is it about that soldier boy in the paper?"

"Yes," I said.

The woman had her face turned towards the sun and she was squinting. Her skin was mottled with sun spots, her neck wrinkled, her clothes shabby. Poor, I thought, and the expression "dirt poor" came to me. The farmers round here are hurting, living a subsistence life, some of them just barely, which is why so many dairy farmers have buckled and sold out to the conglomerates. This woman of German immigrant stock—Helga Schmidt—was hanging on by a gossamer thread.

"I've just picked the last of the Brussel sprouts," she said.

"I didn't know they grew all winter," I said.

"I keep a few things going in the green house over there," she said, and pointed to a ramshackle structure covered with cloudy plastic by the side of her house. I could tell she wanted to keep talking. What else does a farmer have to do on a cold winter day? There were no animals to tend to that I could see, not even a dog or a cat. I think she was alone there and wondered if she was lonely, or if she had children who would take care of her— eventually—though she seemed robust enough.

The Brussels looked fresh and she bagged a few for me. I thanked her and gave her my card. "If you notice anything, or if the family returns, please give me a call," I said. She peered at the card and read it, moving her lips. She hadn't understood. "You the police?" she asked.

"Private Investigator. Didn't I say that before?"

"Not that I heard," she said.

"Give me a call when your neighbors come back," I said again.

I walked back to the RV owner's house for another go around. Despite the cold, there was a half-frozen puddle with leaves swirling on its surface. A car had been standing there until recently, its warm engine melting what lay underneath. But the neighbor hadn't noticed anything, or so she had said.

The blinds were down on the windows, the interior dark. There were no footprints, no garbage, and no evidence of a recent fire. Ice stalactites hung from the branches and a snow covered nineteenth century plow lay on its side in front of the barn which was locked with three locks, the doors tightly sealed. The spaces between the slats were sealed from the inside with black plastic, either an attempt to keep the elements out, or to hide something.

When I returned to the car, the woman—Helga—was there, trespassing on her neighbor's property. Well, so was I. She'd probably been watching me the whole time because she had nothing else to do and was suddenly curious about these neighbors who she had never noticed much before. I worried that she might get too involved. We didn't know anything, as yet, about the people who lived there. I had to warn her without freaking her out or alienating her good intentions. I didn't think I could rely on her to call for help before she raised her own shotgun.

"Find anything?" she asked.

"Not much," I said. "Thanks for your help. I'll cook up these veggies tonight. And, Helga, I'd advise you to stay away from here even if you notice something, especially if you notice something. Just call the police or call me. Do you understand?"

I climbed into my car and spoke to her again through the window because Helga hadn't responded to my request. She hadn't said she understood. "Helga," I said. "Did you hear what I just said to you?"

"It's okay, dear," she said, nearly the same words Mrs. Woolf had uttered when I arrived to tell her about Christa.

CHAPTER 8

Peg had suggested we check in with the Rizzos at regular intervals. We could take turns or go together, as necessary. Mel was cooking up some pasta when I arrived late one day and Barbara was setting the table. Anyone looking in the window might have thought this was a normal household and that I was a regular guest, a friend of the family, a relation. I asked if anything new had occurred to them.

Lights passed across the window as I sat down. The Rizzo's house was set back from the road so where did these lights come from? We began to talk, but my attention wandered from time to time to the flickering in the woods behind the house—a flashlight or a lighter. For the first time, I believed Mel and Barbara. Someone was there.

"The drawing of the disjointed body next to the first bag of bones was similar to the drawings David did when he was a kid," Barbara said.

She let the sentence out in one breath. She had been building her strength to speak and now her strength was compromised again and her breath exhausted. Releasing information piecemeal diluted reality—David had disappeared. And to withhold information was a form of magical thinking, I thought. I had a vision of endless clues buried and then released like confetti into the polluted air of an underground tomb. Maybe we were on an archaeological dig after all. That was one of Barbara Rizzo's throwaway lines the day Charlie Griffith had first interviewed her.

I made a note to talk to Maggie Steed about the Rizzos, their reluctance to share all they knew. If I could figure them out, it might help me in future investigations. I hadn't yet talked to Peg about what I had assumed was her ulterior motive in sending me down to Vassar. I had to let my anger go; Maggie Steed was a useful resource.

I excused myself and went to the bathroom, called Peg to tell her about the lights. "Someone will be there in ten minutes," she said.

"We need to have a serious talk," I said to Mel and Barbara when I returned. "The FBI is on the case, the Patriot Act has been invoked. I'm sure we're all under surveillance. If David is alive and he's done something wrong, we want to make sure he's protected. I'm getting out my notebook and my recorder. Begin with David's first tour overseas. What happened to him?"

"You mean someone could be watching David watching us."

"Exactly."

"Good guys or bad guys?" Mel asked.

"Either, both," I said.

"I don't believe this," Barbara said.

"Who wants to start?"

The shadows between the trees deepened and a twig snapped. Barbara's back was to the window; Mel was at the end of the table facing sideways. I noticed him glancing outside from time to time, but his gaze didn't linger there. His large, soft hands were trembling. They showed no signs of age or use. Barbara was the laborer in the family, the gardener, the one with physical skills. She said, "David's emails to us were short, descriptive of the local people he'd met and the beauty of the landscape, the cradle of civilization, and how it was destroyed."

She spoke eloquently and fluently. The words were hot, like lava.

"He rarely mentioned any deaths or battles," she continued. "He wanted us to know he was okay and not to worry. And then, as we already told you, during his second tour, his emails stopped."

"Anything else? Anything else at all? Did he mention his army buddies by name?"

"Sometimes. But we can't remember who they were," Mel said too quickly.

"Did you keep the emails?"

"They must be on my system. I don't delete anything," Mel said.

I looked outside again, and now there was only blackness, the lights had vanished. The moon was hidden under a thick bank of clouds.

Sergeant De Beyer arrived at the front door. He was in plain clothes, driving an unmarked car. Once again he'd searched the grounds, but found nothing. I hadn't told the Rizzos Peg had called someone other than me to come over and they were alarmed. Any arrival by an official at their house felt ominous. Had David been found? Had his body been found?

"This time I saw something," I told the Sergeant.

"Nothing there," he said. "Let's have another look in daylight, Alison."`

I walked him to his car and put my hand on his arm. Rosie had told me once that a light touch is the best way to get a man's attention. But another call was coming up on his radio and he had to go. It was foolish to get involved with a colleague, of course, and at such a fraught moment, a family inside suffering, but I couldn't stop myself.

* * *

"I've lost my faith," Barbara said.

"In what?" I asked.

"In everything."

"And I feel the opposite," I said. "I am sure that David is still alive."

∗ ∗ ∗

An odd complacency set in. I went home to my cozy new apartment and rested for an afternoon, read and slept. The next morning, someone hacked into an instant message as I was talking to Peg. The message was addressed to me: GET OFF THE RIZZO CASE. WE KNOW WHERE YOU ARE.

"That's a threatening message," Charlie said. "Is there someplace you can stay?"

"I can stay at my friend Rosie's."

"Give me her address and wherever you go, let me know, let Peg know. Agent Dolan wants to see you. I'd suggest you get in here first thing tomorrow morning. Lock up your apartment."

"I'm not quitting."

"I know that, Alison."

I cleaned-up the kitchen, showered with my gun on the toilet seat, packed a bag and left. I drove back to the Rizzo's house, called Sergeant De Beyer, and together we searched the grounds. There were footprints everywhere, a size 11 shoe. They weren't David's.

∗ ∗ ∗

A fleet of trucks was out salt-sanding the roads and the trip over to New Paltz took more than an hour. I listened to the Albany NPR station, a program about sky diving in Australia, summer there. I tried not to think about Christa.

Charlie Griffith was happy to see me; his sincerity was constant. "You remember Special Agent Pat Dolan," he said, as he emptied three chairs of files so we could all sit down. My hand was moist as we shook hands. I needed to take it easy, to observe, to let Peg take the lead whenever possible. I'd had no experience with FBI agents except for the night Pat Dolan had shown up at my apartment uninvited. I assumed there would be continuing attempts to control or oversee our investigation. I concentrated on Agent Dolan's pristine French manicure. I'd never had a manicure, or wanted one. Peg's nails were cut short and her hands were calloused from recent fix-it jobs in her house. Mine and Charlie's were the same. Agent Dolan had abandoned her introductory suit and was dressed informally in slacks and a sweater. This was her day-to-day wardrobe apparently. Peg and I were in jeans, vests and waterproof hiking boots. They stayed on all winter. Charlie was in a suit which didn't quite fit. The bold tie was 1930's deco.

"It's time we had a good talk," Agent Dolan began. "We got off on the wrong foot and I take responsibility for that. Charlie has been telling me about all the good work you've done on this case and others."

"Thanks for that," Peg said.

"What's your intuition?" Agent Dolan asked.

Though she was addressing both of us, we'd agreed that only Peg would speak.

"I'm not a psychic," she began. "I work on the evidence, the clues, follow the trail until I get to the end of it and we've got a resolution, or closure."

"What's the difference?"

"A body, clothes left on the embankment, charred remains, we deduce what's happened, that's resolution. Disappearance without return, a hot trail gone cold, we discuss the most likely scenario based on the evidence we have: abductive forensics. Either way we have closure. You get the picture."

"I do," Agent Dolan said. Her expression altered, I thought, if only for an instant. Everyone has a life, sorrows and joys. I could give her that at least. Or maybe she found Peg's sarcasm annoying.

"How far are you along?" Peg asked. "Are you closing in on David Rizzo or are you closing in on his body?"

"He's alive. I thought you knew that," Pat Dolan said.

"I thought he might be. But where is he?" I asked.

I was struggling not to look surprised, or worried. Peg and Charlie showed no emotion because, I only later realized, they understood that Agent Dolan was fishing, an oblique way of doing business with us.

"We're looking after him. He's in protective custody," she continued.

"When did you pick him up?" Peg asked, poker faced. We all knew David was not in custody.

"Yesterday."

"Can we talk to him? His parents will want to know he is okay," I said.

"That won't be possible," Agent Dolan said.

"And Christa's murder?" Charlie asked.

"Still unsolved. Any ideas?"

"Nothing to share at the moment," Charlie said. "I have someone in protective custody also—Alison. She got a death threat this morning."

"I heard about that. Charlie taking care of you?" she asked turning to face me. She had a pretty face.

"I don't know, are you Charlie?" I asked.

"I am, Alison."

"We'll be in touch soon," Agent Dolan said.

"You bet," Peg said.

The sarcasm hadn't lifted and I was disappointed. It was a sense of honor the war had broken; it remained with me when I judged others. I was like a child who trusts her parents until they let her down. And I was confused by Agent Dolan and how we should cooperate with her, or whether we had to cooperate with her totally. I think Peg's sarcasm signaled her own confusion. Charlie, more mature, didn't flinch throughout the so-called discussion.

I leaned back in the chair hard, heard a spring snap, and came back upright a bit too fast. The action jolted me. This agent had been taught to lie with impunity. The FBI wanted David Rizzo badly, but not necessarily because he'd done anything wrong.

* * *

"What's going on, Charlie?" Peg asked as soon as Agent Dolan had shut the door.

"Wish I knew, Peg. They say they picked David up in a cemetery somewhere. A trooper over near Roscoe called in and asked for an ID on him when he saw the address on his driver's license. He was wearing camouflage and his beret. There's got to be more to it because as soon as Dolan heard he'd been found, she rode out to Sullivan County with her associate to get him."

"And you never saw him?"

"No."

"So it could have been someone else using David Rizzo's identity," I said.

"Yes, of course," Charlie said.

"I think someone is trying to pin Christa's murder on David Rizzo," I continued. "He may be back in Iraq or Afghanistan for all we know. Or he may be dead, someone using his identity. Dolan was bluffing, fishing. The word trust isn't in her vocabulary so we have to assume whatever she says to us also cannot be trusted. Has she been to see Mel and Barbara? I'm sure she has. Mel Rizzo lied to me about David's emails. He said he'd kept them but I don't think he did. His hands were shaking and he spoke haltingly like someone had a gun to his head. His demeanor reminded me of kidnapped private contractors in Iraq—false video confessions—before they are returned to their cells, tortured or beheaded. What's the FBI up to here?"

I was full of theories and needed to slow down. "Maybe the instant message wasn't a threat, maybe it was a code and David is trying to contact me. I'm going home," I said, finally.

"Are you sure?" Charlie asked.

"It doesn't matter where I am. If David Rizzo is alive, he can find me anywhere. He's Special Operations, but I suppose you know that."

"We do," Charlie said.

Charlie got out of his chair and put his hand on my shoulder as if to ground me. I'd been crying inside since the day Christa was killed and now the ocean of fear and sorrow had swelled again and spilled onto my cheeks and neck. Still, I didn't know why Charlie was holding me. What had he seen that I couldn't see or acknowledge?

"It'll be okay Alison," Charlie said. " We're working together. You won't be hurt."

Peg said, "Charlie's right, Alison. I hope you are hearing him. We're in this together." They told me to go home and get some rest. In the army there had never been any rest and I couldn't remember what a restful night was even now. My sleep was often tormented.

I drove home in a fugue state and curled up in bed with all my clothes on. I dreamt I was lying on muddy ground with Anwar and that his intestines were falling out of his stomach and that I couldn't save him. I called Maggie Steed and made an appointment to see her. This time it was for me.

CHAPTER 9

As I stepped into the vestibule, I heard the wide wooden floorboards creak. I put my bag down, took off my boots and locked the door. Broken glass crunched under my feet and it shone under the reflected light from the kitchen. I hadn't expected to see David so soon. He was dressed in full battle gear, a helmet fitted out with night vision on the table. And there was grease around his eyes. As I had thought, Agent Dolan had either lied to us about picking David up, or been fooled into thinking someone else was David. Probably, the former.

A soldier's behavior is predictable in the safety of boot camp, predictable in the field until contact is made with the enemy. After that, every event is unpredictable, all outcomes unforeseen, engagement and retreat equally chaotic. Within hours of our first battle, the dim light of sanity collapses and we lose any expectation that it even exists. Was David sane or insane? Drugged or sober?

"Hello Private Investigator Alison Jenkins," he said.

That sounded normal. I decided to proceed as if it was, that it was perfectly normal to see a soldier in full battle gear in my kitchen. Otherwise, the emptiness of the space was palpable, the apartment barely furnished, no plants. I was a woman living alone eager to live on my own, but I missed the boisterous voices of my family around the dinner table, Charlie's gentle touch, and Peg's patience. I hoped they were nearby, as promised.

"David," I said. "You've broken into my email. You've broken into my apartment."

"All for a good cause, Alison, all for a good cause," he said.

His voice was shallow. He had never smoked and now, as he spoke, it was as though he were singing a refrain from a pop tune. I did not ask what the good cause might be because I would have to say to him very soon that his parents were waiting, that he would have to call them, or that I would. That was a fact David could not avoid though I understood now that his disappearance had been deliberate.

I went to the refrigerator and pulled out a couple of beers, set them on the table. I felt as though we were back in high school about to spend an evening together shooting the breeze. How could we erase the intervening years and Christa's murder? I took out my gun and put it on the table. It would be useless against the guns—two of them—David was carrying, or his pumped-up arms, but I wanted him to know I was prepared to use my gun.

"I missed you that day we were supposed to sketch together," I said.

"It couldn't be helped," David said. "I was sure you'd understand."

"I didn't," I said, which wasn't entirely true. I'd given him slack, forgiven what I interpreted then as a warrior's walkabout, and gone off to sketch on my own.

His left eye twitched and I saw that it was bruised under the grease, a fighter's bruise. Someone had punched him.

"What happened to your eye?" I asked

"I ran into a branch. It happens."

"Why don't I believe you?" I said.

"I am glad you are my friend, Alison. I will tell you why I am here. I have decided to explain everything. I would like to speak to a reporter. Can you find a reporter?"

"We have to discuss Christa," I said.

"You probably think I killed her."

"Did you kill her?"

"You have got to know that I did not kill her, Alison. I loved her. There is so much to explain. Can you find me a reporter?"

"I will try," I said. "But you cannot threaten me anonymously again, and we must call your parents to let them know you are alive."

The room dimmed with apprehension. David stood up and gathered his helmet and his guns. They clattered against each other as he dragged himself to the door. He had an injured leg or foot; dried blood sprawled across the camouflage near the top of his right combat boot. He turned to face me and said again that he would like to speak to a reporter.

"How will I get in touch with you?" I asked.

"Leave that to me," he said.

And then he was gone.

I did not dare to follow him out the door because I did not want to stop him from contacting me again. I called Peg, but her cell went into voice mail. Charlie was out of the office. After a half-hour or so, I walked down to the end of my driveway and then around the house, but there was no sign of David anywhere or of any unmarked cars patrolling. I thought: how is Charlie Griffith protecting me as he said he would? I am here on my own. But, once again, I was mistaken. Charlie was behind the house next door with Peg and two troopers. And all of us had made the decision in concert, without discussion, that we would let David go because he would lead us to Christa's killer.

* * *

My dreams were full of bodies. The bodies were in the water floating into each other and they were all faceless and gray with mildew. There was no blood, no sign of mutilation or combat. The dreams woke me and I recorded them in a book so I could discuss them with the psychologist Maggie Steed had referred me to. But the writing didn't help me get back to sleep. I visualized a peaceful scene: Buddha sitting under a cherry tree, petals drifting in a light wind onto the hallowed ground. But that didn't help either. I hadn't called the psychologist to make my first appointment. I suppose it was time. Maggie thought it was time. I turned on the light and picked up the Trollope, ate a banana, sipped on some so-called relaxing tea, and eventually got back to sleep. Three hours later the alarm went off. I was battle ready in ten minutes and on the road to Mel and Barbara's by 9 a.m. I stopped at a Stewart's for a coffee, called a reporter I knew and left a message. I was feeling hopeful again.

* * *

The Rizzos had received a visit from Agent Pat Dolan. It had not been a threatening visit and she had been kind to them, respectful, Mel and Barbara told me. In this way, she had gained their confidence and cooperation. They had offered her refreshments and sat at the kitchen table where we always sat when I was there. It was as though the rest of the house had been closed off and life reduced to its fundamentals: a place to eat, a place to sleep. When I arrived, Mel was in the back-garden chopping wood. It was the one task he could do that Barbara was incapable of doing. He stacked the wood and then took a few logs into the side of the house where there was a separate entrance to his office. It was a Sunday afternoon and the town had been deserted as I drove through it, all the shops closed, very little traffic. The Rizzo's house was tranquil also, but it was not a natural Sunday tranquility. I did not take off my down vest. The kitchen was cold.

At first, my voice was full of mock optimism, but I could not sustain this for very long. I began with the assurance that David had not killed Christa. I did not yet tell them he was alive or had been in my apartment. I just said that I knew he had not killed Christa. They were relieved and we all fell silent again. Then Barbara made some coffee and laid out a plate of oatmeal cookies she had baked that morning. Mel said, "Agent Dolan seems to think David is still alive." This was my opening and I took it.

"He was in my apartment," I said, as gently as possible.

Mel got out of his chair slowly and turned his back to the table. He walked over to the glass doors leading to the garden and he opened the door. The cold air filled the room and the room was now frigid. There was, of course, more I had to say, more I had to explain.

"Mel, please sit down so we can talk," I said.

Barbara was clutching her cup and she was weeping quietly. Then she got up and she threw the cup into the sink where it shattered.

I sat at the table patiently. I had learned this particular kind of patience from Peg, from Charlie, and from my friend, Rosie. She had become a Buddhist and had taken me to a temple in Woodstock to meditate occasionally. I practiced remaining calm and did not move or speak for a very long time. Finally, both Mel and Barbara sat down and I settled enough within myself so that I could explain.

"David is alive," I began. "But he is also in danger. He came to ask if I knew a reporter I trust. I have already called a reporter, a man I met in Iraq. David is injured, but not badly injured. The wound is dry, but there are blood stains on his pants and he is limping. His eye was bruised. He has probably been in a fight."

I decided not to mention the battle gear as this would only alarm them further. It wasn't a necessary detail.

"And you let him go? You could not stop him or capture him?" Mel asked. "You could not bring him here?"

"We want to him to lead us to Christa's killer," I said.

But this simple explanation wasn't enough for Mel whose mental geography had shifted when his son had disappeared. He had once been a rational man, a psychologist. But he had lost the habit of methodical thought and was now unmoored. I understood and I remained patient, until the storm of misery receded. I needed more information from Mel and Barbara about Agent Dolan's visit.

"We will sue you if anything more happens to our son," Mel said. "And we will sue the FBI."

A sad hush followed this outburst.

"You have hired us to help you," I said. "As for the FBI, I cannot speak for their involvement. Frankly, Peg and I, even Charlie Griffith, don't entirely understand why they are here."

"Agent Dolan was interested in any papers David might have stored here. I told her there was nothing."

"And is that true?"

"I have some boxes in the cellar stored in fire boxes behind the boiler," Mel said. "David told me not to touch them."

"I didn't know anything about this," Barbara said with irritation.

"I just remembered," Mel said.

Either his memory had been anesthetized by anxiety—not unusual—or he was trying to protect Barbara.

"I'll get Charlie and Peg over here to have a look. Can you keep this from Agent Dolan, Mel?"

"She will find out sooner or later," he said.

"That may be true. But let's hold her off until we have studied what is there. We do not have the same agenda, Mel. Agent Dolan works for the government and we work for you."

I could see that Mel Rizzo did not find my explanations comforting and that his internal doors were shut securely. Doubt in the investigation had replaced trust. I reiterated my optimism, my conviction: David had been trained at the Army Special Operations Command Center at Fort Bragg. He had been taught to survive for months at a time in adverse conditions, clandestinely, or in the open. He had learned to forage for food and shelter; he had learned to stay warm when it is cold and cold when it is warm. He had worked as a medic, an expert in communications, and an expert in counter-terrorism. A soldier so highly trained does not wait for orders to act. He was in pursuit and it was our job to let him do his job and to follow him.

"David is alive," Barbara said.

It had taken her a long time to digest the news. Her face now had no expression—neither anger, nor irritation, nor despair. She went over to the sink and cleaned up the broken cup. Then she went upstairs without saying good-bye.

CHAPTER 10

Charlie Griffith was working on a new case which he thought might be related to David's disappearance and Christa's murder. A seamstress serving the university community in New Paltz had been brutally raped and murdered. Most of her clientele were professors with skirts to hem, sleeves to shorten, rips to be mended, elbows to be patched, and buttons to be replaced. All with alibis and most definitely innocent, Charlie said. The woman had survived the attack long enough to describe the scene of her own murder in eccentric, vibrant detail: "He come at me with a hatchet. I kicked him but he still come at me. Blood flowed around me. I could not dream."

No one in the emergency room could comprehend her ability to speak, but speak she did. She did not say she recognized the man only that it was a man, a big man, who had struck the blow. He left the murder weapon next to her body, his fingerprints smeared away with her blood. Bloody shoe prints circled her body, ritualistically patterned on the slate floor. Size 11 combat boots with worn threads, the same-sized shoe print that Ed De Beyer and I had found behind the Rizzo's house.

But why a hatchet, Charlie wanted to know.

Twischawkin, the land where plums abound. This is how the indigenous people of the Hudson Valley once described their home before the invaders came. Historians have written about their lives, the shift from the Lenape language to Dutch, from Dutch to English. And because the seamstress had been murdered with a hatchet, two contemporary historians of Native American lore and history suggested that the police search out Native inhabitants on the reservations and land trusts further north.

"Let's keep our eye on the soldiers," I said.

"One of the soldiers could be Native," Peg said. "There are many serving."

"Or it could be a diversion," Charlie said.

Two unsolved murders, a killer or killers still at large, and David Rizzo was still missing, still disappeared. And though both murders were brutal, local interest peaked and then fell away with the first melt of spring. Even the professors who had lobbied the police and written editorials for the local papers eulogizing the dead seamstress lost interest as the end of term approached. By the time the cherry blossoms blossomed and fell, and the Wallkill River surged into the flood plain, David Rizzo's disappearance and the two unsolved murders had vanished from the local papers and from chance conversations. Any fear of a killer residing nearby dissipated in the balmy, scented air. Corn was planted, sunflowers. The farm stands opened to sell root vegetables and apples stored in barns over the winter. Sentences began, "Do you remember the ice storm?" and everyone told a story about the biggest storm among many we had that winter: the downed power lines, the trees laden with freeze, branches snapping, detours away from the slick roads in the mountains, the wonder and beauty of the ice forest glittering in the sun in the days following the storm.

I never could understand the capacity to forget so easily. I reassured the Rizzos that our work continued and downplayed the presence of the FBI. They were keeping a low profile, or were so adept at deep background that we rarely noticed them. We worked tirelessly following up leads, hopeful one day, pessimistic the next.

And because David had appeared in my apartment, we put a stop order on the dredging of the river.

And then, one day, the burlap bag family returned to the farm on Rte. 28 near Phoenicia. Law enforcement in all fifty states had not been able to locate them yet now they were back, or had never left. Helga Schmidt had called and said, simply: "They're back." I reiterated my instructions to keep away and she promised me she would. In most people, survival instincts are stronger than curiosity. I hoped that would be the case with Helga and that my warning had been strong enough.

Peg wasn't sure I should go on my own, nor was Charlie. But I said I'd be okay and would call for back-up immediately if I needed any. It was just a first foray, an exploration. Who were these people? What was their connection, if any, to Christa's murder, to the bags of bones, or to David? Maybe the bags had been stolen by one of their workers and they, too, were innocent. I kept my suspicions at bay as I pulled into the parking area in front of the farm stand. Plastic sheeting had been pulled up onto the roof and a man and a woman, elderly or old beyond their years, short in stature like European peasants, struggled to unload a burlap bag of potatoes into a bushel basket. The empty bags were piled under the rickety wooden tables.

I was the only one there; traffic is sparse most days on Rte. 28 until the tourist season begins. I said hello, introduced myself, pulled out my ID. The man shoved the woman aside with his forearm. "She doesn't speak English," he said in near perfect English and then he told the woman to go into the house, in Russian. In retrospect that was the moment I should have excused myself and called for back-up. But I was on a roll and couldn't stop, my instincts driving me forward into a danger zone. And I wasn't in a Humvee with my buddies behind me; I was alone.

"I'm interested in those potato bags of yours," I said, pointing to the pile under the table. "They've been turning up in strange places with bones inside them."

"I don't know anything. You the police? The FBI? What?"

I showed him my ID again. "Private Investigator," I said again. "We're investigating the disappearance of a soldier, David Rizzo. Know him?"

"I don't have to talk to you."

"I suggest you answer my questions," I said. "The police will be here soon enough. We are working together."

Somebody turned on a light in the house behind translucent shades but all I could see were shadows: the old woman, a couple of men, and a child. Why did I feel so edgy? I probably should not have mentioned David Rizzo.

"What did you say your name was?" I asked.

"Popov. Vladimir Popov."

His voice was flat, gravely, like an old woman who had smoked most of her life. A woman's voice deepens with age, a man's distorts. Vladimir Popov was coughing and couldn't stop. I took out my notebook, pretended to jot some notes. It was another missed opportunity to get into my car and onto the radio.

"Do you have any grandchildren?" I asked.

I had seen a child in the shadows and hoped he or she would be a grandchild.

"I have two sons," he said.

"And where are they, Mr. Popov?"

"One is in Afghanistan working for NATO, one is dead," he replied, deadpan.

"I'm sorry. Did your son die overseas?"

"He died in Baghdad."

I was about to give up in my attempt to get any real information. Vladimir Popov, a common enough Russian name, true, but I had heard it before, or perhaps read it in a newspaper article. I stalled for more time and asked again about the bags. I asked if any were missing, a ridiculous question. What farmer keeps careful count of his bags?

"Has anyone been staying here while you've been away for the winter?" I asked.

"Many people."

"Many people?"

"Family. Friends."

It wasn't a good sign that Vladimir Popov continued to lie and that I persisted in questioning him knowing he was lying. Helga Schmidt was not a foolish woman. If anyone had come to stay in the house, she would have noticed. There was no doubt that the house and barn were in use, but not during the day. The locks on the barn were not iced over and probably had been opened and closed regularly. Whoever had been there had been stealthy, had arrived in the dead of night, and had left before Helga was awake.

"I didn't notice anyone in the house, or any cars, whenever I passed here," I said.

"Perhaps they didn't take us up on our offer."

The lights in the house were wavering, shadows moving swiftly from one side of the room to the other. The door swung open and a man in camouflage rushed onto the porch and down the stairs. He grabbed me by the neck and pulled me inside. A young girl, no more than ten-years-old, a black scarf folded in a box-like shape around her head, was sitting on the floor, her head rolling onto her chest. She was drugged. Next to her was another soldier with his chin on his hands. He might have been praying or sleeping.

I was shoved against the wall and told not to move.

"Is this your boy who died in Baghdad?" I asked Vladimir Popov.

"What an amateur you are," he said to me.

Then the woman spoke. "Shut up," Vladimir Popov said to her, but she did not shut up. I heard the word gun and the name Boris. The man with the gun who had pulled me inside by the neck was her son. She was telling him to put the gun down. Then she went over to the young girl, took her hand, and walked with her into a back room. I thought: If there is anyone I must save it is the young girl. But how would I save her without backup? My gun was in the glove compartment of the car, but even if it had been in the small of my back, what good would it have done?

They weren't going to shoot me, not yet anyway. They would want to know exactly who I was and if anyone knew I was there. Then the young girl came back into the room by herself and lay down on the floor by the wood stove. She had a beatific smile on her face. I felt nauseous imaging what they'd done to her, what they'd done to Christa, what they'd done to the seamstress. The murders—Christa and the seamstress—this drama, holding me hostage, the girl, the burlap bags with bones, all connected. I'd almost forgotten about David in the midst of the delusion that I was Superwoman.

The room was very warm and I wanted to take off my denim jacket. I cannot move well if I am too warm. I had learned that in Iraq; my legs were molasses the whole time I was there. It wasn't only the heavy gear, it was the sweat that gathered inside our uniforms and the rank odor of our bodies that wore us down before we could get into a shower.

A log in the wood stove hissed and then collapsed. Every sound in the house was magnified. I studied the men's faces, grease around their eyes, stubble on their cheeks, brown-stained teeth. They looked deranged. Their uniforms were shredded at the knees and elbows, the combat boots dulled by dirt and scuffs. The second soldier spit between his feet, bent over, and said something to the girl in Farsi or Dari, the related languages of Iran and Afghanistan. His tone was kind, solicitous, all a façade because the girl was hostage, too.

"Who's the girl?" I asked.

"An orphan," Boris Popov said. His English was perfect. He had certainly been born in America or arrived at an early age. He looked like Vladimir, like father like son, rough and cruel.

"And what do you plan to do with her?" I asked him.

"That's none of your business," he said.

"So you've been to Afghanistan?"

"Shut her up," Vladimir Popov said.

"How long do you think you can hold me here?" I asked.

I glanced out the window. It was getting dark. The driveway wrapped around the house like a snake. A black car was parked in front of the RV. I hadn't seen it from the road.

The girl had to use the bathroom. The old woman called her Fatima, a common name, and probably not her real name. She escorted her to the back of the house and when they returned, they were holding hands. *Fatima, I will save you,* I thought. She curled up in front of the stove again and fell asleep, her thin ankles poking out of a long brown skirt.

"I'm not the police or the FBI," I said. "I'm a private investigator working for the Rizzo family. Do you know David Rizzo?"

"The best officer," Boris Popov said.

"Have you seen David? Talked to him? That's my only interest here. Whatever you are doing, as you say, is none of my business. Tell me about David and I won't call the cops on you."

"We hear Rizzo washed up somewhere," Boris Popov said.

"Washed up? Drowned?"

"Turned up," the second soldier said.

"Can you tell me anything else?"

"No," Vladimir said.

I struggled to a standing position. My knees cracked. I hadn't worked out in a while.

"I have to be going," I said.

I was on an adrenalin high, immortal. It was the only way to explain my decision to get up and turn towards the door, my back to these violent men. I opened the door slowly, closed it, and walked to my car. No footsteps, no door flying open. I heard a loud bang—possibly a gunshot—as I pulled away and drove south at high speed towards Woodstock. I called Peg from the ice cream parlor on Main Street. I needed something sweet. They had probably put a bullet in the young girl's head.

CHAPTER 11

During my PI training, I had noticed that poor people, criminals, addicts and ex-cons hang out at Laundromats and all-night mini-mart gas stations where there are bathrooms, a plentiful supply of beer, candy and sandwiches, and a table or two to sit down. The proprietors in upstate New York these days are mostly from the Indian sub-continent, Bengalis or Sikhs. Depending on their education, they speak English well, a legacy of colonialism. The family works and lives together in an extension of the communal life they had in Asia. This is their new home and they are a new species of American—ambitious and entrepreneurial—with global identities. They may carry dual citizenship and their children become hip Americans within one generation. Any lingering loyalties these children have to their parents' country of origin evaporate in the seductive, often illusory atmosphere of America's bounty and opportunity. Their parents remain ambivalent, skeptical or cynical about American mores, tied to ancestry and tradition; their longings for home do not subside. Often, there is conflict between the generations and it is painful. I knew one such family and filled up at their gas station whenever I was in the neighborhood. One of the sons had gone into the army and was killed within a month of his tour in Afghanistan. The second son, Gavin, was still in college, living at home, and was working at the cash desk when I pulled in after my ice cream feast in Woodstock. Observant and articulate, he had become one of my informers while I was studying to be a PI and sent out on an assignment to find reliable informers. There was no one more reliable than a boy like Gavin, eager to please and do well in life. And the fact that I had been a soldier, and returned alive, also meant a lot to him and the family. They were heartbroken when their eldest son was killed and couldn't understand why he'd enlisted. I deflected questions about how he had died, not a question I could answer because I wasn't there and, even if I had been there, the moment of his death might have been obscured in smoke and rubble. "Valiantly," the messenger had said when he arrived with the sad news. "I am sure he died bravely," I said often reinforcing a lasting image every parent should have of their dead soldier child. Our discussions, always short and in the middle of transactions, eventually became warm and philosophical: the meaning of war, the meaning of death in war and, with each visit, I stayed longer and sometimes sat at a table with them as an honored guest. "Alison is here," Gavin or his father or mother would say as I walked in, calling to each other from the front of the shop to the back office.

It had been a slow day and Gavin was happy to see me. His parents had already gone home to rest and prepare dinner. The radio was on to a local station and there was a report that troopers had arrived at a farm house on Rte. 28 and had set up a detour. When Gavin asked if I knew what was going on, I told him some of it hoping that a customer might have spilled a bit of news I could use. I was feeling pretty bad thinking about the young girl on the floor in the long brown skirt, how thin she was, how I couldn't save her, and how I had made a fatal mistake in not calling for back up right away. Gavin said, "You look a bit desperate, Alison." The boy hardly knew me and he was still young, yet he had understood. His parents' wisdom had touched him and he wasn't like other boys his age, my own fun-loving brothers, for example.

I asked him if he had noticed any soldiers around lately or anything that made him suspicious. He said he'd think about it. He poured me a strong cup of home-brewed tea from the large brown pot; it was invigorating. My eyes were swollen with unshed tears, the after-shock of the incident at the farm, and too much sugar—in the ice cream, in the tea—made me shaky. For the first time in many years of not smoking, I wanted a cigarette. I had not even smoked in Iraq and now the packs of cigarettes behind the counter were beckoning.

Gavin said he would call me if he thought of anything or anyone, and I left. I sat in the car for a while, took out my notebook and made a list of dangling clues: the documents in the Rizzo house, the size 11 shoeprint behind the Rizzo's house and at the scene of the seamstress' murder, the young Iranian or Afghani girl—yet to be determined, Mrs. Woolf, the scene at the farmhouse, David's request to meet with a reporter. I had called the reporter—Mike Fuller—right away and left messages. I was avoiding Peg, avoiding Charlie. It had already been a long day but I couldn't or wouldn't rest. I called Mike Fuller again. He was home and invited me over. I put the notebook on the passenger seat, took some deep breaths, and inched my way onto the darkening road, the shoulder a porous border leading into the wilderness. I caught a deer in my headlights, stopped, honked to frighten it away, but it stood paralyzed for a while, unable to move forward or backward in time or space. An oncoming car approached, I flashed my lights, and it stopped also, both cars suspended as the deer—a young stag with its horns not yet fully formed—hesitated , looked around, and then skipped back into the forest.

When I arrived at Mike's log cabin, he was on the screened-in porch planting seedlings of lettuce, tomatoes and kale from small pots to bigger ones, and I offered to help him as we talked. The last time we'd seen each other was at the FOB in Iraq where I'd fed him the story about the barefoot, low-paid workers. He'd never used it which didn't mean he never would. He was a thorough reporter and gathered details carefully before he went to print. And he never relied on press hand-outs to meet his deadlines. We became friends in a way that friendships are formed on the front— casually—but when we discovered that we lived near each other we promised to meet up for a hike some time. Then we ran into each other again during a rail-trail clean-up in New Paltz and swapped phone numbers, but never followed-up. There was sexual attraction, for me at least, but I'd let it go once I understood that the excitement of the front lines is a war reporter's primary passion. Soldiers come home; reporters never do unless they are injured or dead or too old to move quickly in the field. Mike was older than me by five or ten years, I couldn't tell. Certainly, he was nowhere near retirement though he'd been injured more than once. I admired everything about him: his talkative nature, his easy affection for people, and his energy. He was more handsome than I remembered him: lanky and tall with a shock of thick salt and pepper hair falling into his amber eyes. He brushed it back with long fingers. I know I'm in trouble when I begin to notice a man's hands and lips even when I tell myself it's hopeless because the desire isn't reciprocated. I wasn't sure with Mike and was in a state of high alert and high anxiety anyway, no time to be coming on to anyone unless I didn't care about a future with them.

"It sounds like a big story," he said when I told him about David's disappearance and the men at the farm house. He knew who they were right away.

"Boris Popov, let's start with him: Six months in the brig for raping an 11-year-old Iraqi girl. When he got out he signed on with OUTSOURCE, a mercenary organization used by the United States government for jobs they/we don't want to do or are legally prevented from doing."

"That might explain the FBI's interest," I said. "David has stored some documents in his parents' house."

"The FBI won't take long to get their hands on those unless you stash them away first."

I hoped that Peg had already thought of that. I knew that Charlie couldn't with Agent Dolan sitting on his shoulder. But I wished that Charlie Griffith would find a way to help David Rizzo and that Mike Fuller would also.

I began to feel comfortable sitting next to Mike on the porch sipping on beer and talking as though the idea of war had finally been abandoned. I tipped my head to look at the stars, leaned it against the slats of the wooden rocker, and nearly fell asleep. The trees were swaying in a light wind. It had been a long day and I was tipsy. I was about to ask for some coffee so I could drive when Mike got up out of his chair and held out his hand. It was like a boy asking a girl to dance at a prom and it was irresistible to me. "Will you talk to David?" I asked. And he said, "Yes." I trusted him to do what he said he would do. But when and how would David contact me again? And how would I get through the night with Mike Fuller making love to me if I decided to stay? And how would I say goodbye to him in the morning and remain as casual as we had always been? We weren't on the front any more. At least, I wasn't. I knew it would be a one-night stand, and then another, and perhaps another. But that would be it. He could leave without saying good-bye and I'd have to accept his sudden departures, his high-risk occupation, and his promiscuity.

The bed in the corner of his cabin was unmade, the dark gray duvet hanging to the floor and I passed it by quickly when I came out of the bathroom. I didn't violate his medicine cabinet or study his choice of towels. I wasn't planning to stay. I knew what I'd tell Rosie: that I was there on business, that I was being smart, that another night without sex was no big deal, that Mike Fuller was a hunk, but that I didn't want to get involved with him.

The day which had started badly enough suddenly got worse. I got into my car and Mike leaned down into the open window and kissed me good-bye on the lips. "That's for the future," he said. "I'll get in touch with you when I hear from David," I said. Inexplicably, the memory of war was on me again as I drove over the river. Two hawks hovered. Like death, their flight path is wide and now it was following me, stopping my life-affirming impulse to make love to a man I wanted to know better.

* * *

When I arrived home there was an open burlap bag with bones waiting for me at my front door. I knew by now that this was David Rizzo's calling card, but I was not alarmed. I was also certain that he was being tracked and that he had led his stalkers to my door.

I lifted the bag slowly, poured the bones onto the sisal mat, and left them there. In the distance, perhaps 100 meters away, the length of two Olympic swimming pools, a camp fire smoldered. A crude lean-to had been erected next to the fire. I was sure Charlie and his troopers knew it was there. I opened my cell phone: two messages. One from Peg, "Don't go home." Another from Charlie Griffith, "Don't go home." One mistake a day was enough. I must now look after myself if I am to help solve this case, I thought, so I turned around, got back into my car, floored the accelerator, and did not stop until I arrived at Rosie's house. I must have been going 60, 70, 80 miles per hour. I wanted the police to stop me, to take me in, to throw me in jail for the night where I imagined I might be protected. I was in agony about the girl in the long brown skirt. I drove and drove in circles until I was certain no one was on my tail. I hid the car in a stand of trees and walked up to Rosie's house. Like Peg's it was set back in the woods. Light from a crescent moon sliced through the moist air. I was breathless as I knocked on the door, breathless and as frightened as I had been as a child every Halloween night and in the fun house at the amusement park and when I played hide and seek with my brothers. I had been terrified going into battle for the first time, too, of course, but it was a different terror; it had a purpose and I was with other soldiers. We were barely adults, we carried weapons, we weren't alone, and it was an adventure. This was not an adventure; the days of adventure were over.

"I want you to shadow me from now on," Peg said when I called her from Rosie's. "You're not ready to be out on your own. What was I thinking?"

"I have to let David know about Mike Fuller," I said. "He's agreed to talk to him."

"But how will you get in touch with David, Alison? Be sensible."

"I can't do anything more than I am doing, Peg," I said. "I must go back to my apartment so David can contact me somehow. I don't think he was waiting for me. It was someone else. One of the Russians would have known how to scare me well enough. I've got my gun. And Charlie and his troopers can help me out can't they?"

It was almost funny talking this way and I giggled, but it was only nerves.

"We'll discuss this in person first thing tomorrow morning," Peg said. "Please stay the night at Rosie's. That's an order."

"Copy that," I said.

"The parents—Vladimir Popov and his wife—were taken in for questioning. The others have disappeared," Peg continued, "but they are out there and they are dangerous. I don't have to tell you that, Alison."

"What about the girl?" I asked though I knew the answer. Still, I wanted to clear up the fuck-up, what I'd done. There would have to be some penance though I had no idea what that would consist of. Since I'd been a teenager, I had never been to church except on Christmas. It was mostly boredom that had driven me away.

"She's dead," Peg said in such an off-hand way that she might have been talking about a fish. A fish had been pulled out of the water and been slapped into deadness so that we could eat it. My father was a fisherman and I had seen him kill many fish with a quick knock to the head with a rock he'd picked up on the riverbank. It seemed more immediate and, in some ways, crueler than shooting unknown, unseen targets with high powered rifles, I told myself. To hold a fish and strike it until it was dead. The girl was like a fish, cold and vulnerable, killed at close range with a bullet in her back or between her eyes. And why did they have to kill her? She had looked half-dead anyway.

I had been sitting on Rosie's couch talking on my cell phone. I let it slip to the floor and then I fell forward into a faint. Rosie was in the kitchen preparing me something to eat and she heard me keel over. I had never fainted before and I came around quickly. Then I phoned Peg back but did not tell her that I had fainted. It would be another mark against my future as a private investigator.

The next morning I called my therapist and asked if I could come in to see her before my scheduled appointment. But she had no openings. So I went over to Peg's and we sat and we talked. I called Mike Fuller and told him I'd let him know as soon as David contacted me again, but he said, "David Rizzo's already contacted me, Alison." And that was the end of it. He retreated into journalistic privilege and wouldn't say any more: whether he'd talked with David on the phone or in person, or what he had learned. It would be torturous for his parents to hear that David had turned up again and disappeared again. Peg didn't want to call them and she asked me to do it. This time, I refused to be the bearer of hard news.

"What if we encouraged him to come out into the open?" I asked her. "Wouldn't he be safer?"

"If you can find him and hold him, let me know," Peg said.

"And you won't let me out of your sight? I'm in some sort of custody?"

"That's childish, Alison, unworthy of you. You just need closer supervision. I am worried about you. You could have been killed, too. You're too deep in."

"In what?"

"You know what I mean. I hope you change your mind about going to see the Rizzos. Get grounded. Do what you have to do, Alison."

So I said good-bye to Peg and drove down to see Mel and Barbara in a jeep Peg had stored in her barn. It was my turn to use a stealth weapon, to throw whoever was following me off my trail for a few hours, Peg said. I doubted it would work, but I didn't mind driving the jeep.

* * *

It was raining lightly as I pulled into the Rizzo's driveway, a light rain that muddied the ground and quickly evaporated. I rang the bell, no answer, then I walked around to the back. The sliding glass doors overlooking Barbara's well-tended garden were wet and they were open. The rain intensified and dripped in sheets off the gutters and onto the kitchen floor as I stepped inside. Barbara and Mel were not in the house and it looked as though they'd left in a hurry, clothes on the floor, unwashed dishes in the sink, beds unmade. The shower curtain was thrown back and the floor flooded. They would never have left it this way. I was sure the documents Mel told me about would not be in the house any more, that they, too, had been taken. I was sure that Mel and Barbara had been taken.

It might be a crime scene, it might not, Peg reminded me. "Stay there until the cops arrive." It didn't feel right to sit in the house so I waited in my car. I sketched. I listened to the radio. I waited what seemed a long time. I was good at waiting. There wasn't any obvious urgency. Then the cops arrived and looked around. No one uttered the word kidnapping yet except for me. I knew they had been kidnapped, was certain of it. I wanted to turn the investigation around to the beginning and start again. Or call the psychic and go searching for cairns.

CHAPTER 12

Charlie Griffith missed his 11 a.m. appointment with us at the office. A fire was sweeping through the Minnewaska Preserve just west of New Paltz. In less than two hours, more than 3,000 acres had burned. No one was injured, no property was destroyed. But all the hikers, campers and park personnel were evacuated, the road over the mountain shut down. As the most senior officer on duty, Charlie was present throughout the ordeal. At a roadblock he set up just past one of the lay-bys near the West Trapps Trail Head, he spotted a young man with dark, long hair in jeans and a denim jacket. He was leaning against a tree. This man wasn't a trooper, he wasn't a local volunteer fire fighter, and he wasn't anyone Charlie knew from the State Department of Environmental Conservation. He called Peg and asked us to drive over. He had a suspicion about the man and wanted me to identify him. Then he got into his unmarked SUV and rolled downhill to the tree where the man was standing. He pulled in quickly, the bumper resting on the man's hips, just shy of crushing him. Charlie got out of the car and asked the man to turn around and put his hands on the roof. The man didn't move. He asked again. The man smiled. Charlie pulled his gun out of his shoulder holster and shoved it into the man's face. He slid away like a snake before Charlie could even ask him for his ID.

I had never seen Charlie frustrated or angry before. He couldn't understand what had happened. He was strong, he was well trained, but this man was a shape shifter and he couldn't grab him. As he moved off, Charlie told him to halt, but he kept walking west on the road. Then he swung right and disappeared into the woods, but not before Charlie winged him on his left thigh. He was sure he saw the man's hand go down onto the wound and limp away, then he lost sight of him. Two hours of searching with dogs and nothing, not even tracks with blood. We kept Charlie company for a while, discussed the Rizzos, the possibility of a kidnapping, but we weren't in a hurry that day. Every minute without another body or disappearance was pure gain.

"We had to let the Popovs go," he said. "They wouldn't talk and the FBI wouldn't let us charge them."

"So they are on the loose again, also," I said.

Back at Charlie's office, a forensics report was on the desk: The bones in the burlap bags were old, stripped clean, dug up from graves at local cemeteries. We were not displeased that the obvious had been confirmed; the bones were not from fresh bodies, they were toys or metaphors. A morbid metaphor, Maggie Steed explained, when I had first discussed the burlap bags with her. "Perhaps the soldier wants to climb into the grave. Instead, he digs it up. Death in life or brought back to life."

I visualized David scouring grave yards and questioned how he chose the graves he cracked open and how he managed to accomplish the grisly task on his own. Did he use a shovel? An ax? Was the earth loamy or stale? Did the coffin breathe as it was opened? Did the cadaver sigh? And why do we use coffins? In Iraq, Muslim mourners wrap their dead in linen and slip the body into a grave within twenty-four hours. In India, there are funeral pyres. In America, vast cemeteries, often costly to maintain, or cremation, and after cremation, urns. Ashes to ashes, dust to dust. Many former soldiers have found comfort there; the suicide rate among former soldiers is high. Charlie said, "If David is digging up graves, it's a misdemeanor, nothing more. It's not murder. It's not kidnapping."

"Found art," I said. "David's an artist. He's creating sculptures out of rocks, bags and bones."

I hardly knew what I was saying or if it made any sense to anyone else. I was inside David's soldier head and thought I understood him perfectly, why he'd gone to war and had stood by Christa. I was babbling like the birds outside the window. A rush of warm air stirred the papers on Charlie's desk, the forensic report, paper napkins, the folders. Peg took out a brown wax paper bag of sliced apples—her staple and mine—and passed it round. The apples were over-ripe, pulpy and sweet. It was the season for melons and grapes, not for apples. "These have been stored in barns all winter," I said. It would be summer soon. I drifted off into a morbid reverie again. This had been happening to me lately. Instead of nightmares, I had day-time reveries which were worse; they broke my concentration. My therapist told me not to worry, it was only natural that memories would surface in this way. I had to be patient with myself, she said. But it wasn't always possible. Either someone was missing, or someone was dead, a murderer at large. And I couldn't ease up.

"We must get up to the reservation," Charlie said.

There was no need to reply. The man in the preserve was Native. He had long, black unbraided hair, held back by a bandana across his forehead, Charlie said.

"Was he in fatigues?" Peg asked.

"No, denim," Charlie said.

I remembered the second soldier in the house. Could it be the same man? His presence was more fleeting and I had been focused on Boris, his gun, and the girl. The soldiers' faces were covered in grease which framed their eyes like masks. I could not remember many details about their appearance except for their ragged uniforms and scuffed boots. They were like characters in an action movie whose gestures threaten violence in every frame.

Charlie said again, "We have to get up to the reservation."

Having said this twice, Peg began to take it seriously. "We will make our plans tomorrow, Charlie."

It would mean a day away, a bit of a break for all of us as we drove up and back together.

* * *

The Oneida Indian Nation Police Department, based in Canastota New York, near Syracuse is a professionally trained law enforcement agency empowered by the sovereign authority of the Oneida Indian Nation. Members of the force are deputized by federal authority and work closely with state and federal authorities. They do not have jurisdiction over non-Indians in criminal cases. If Boris Popov or any of his gang were hiding out on the reservation, a state trooper could arrest them. So could the FBI. "I haven't heard from Agent Dolan recently," Charlie said. He didn't seem disappointed. Nor did he say that he was keeping her in the loop as she had requested. So we made our own plans and headed north not knowing what we would find there. Charlie had only recently discovered that the murdered seamstress was Oneida. Were the tribal police missing something? Or protecting someone as we were protecting David? I'd had a couple of Native friends in the army. They were the best trackers, steady as rails. Traditional or urban, they were all heir to displacement. I thought of Gavin and his family, their transplantation to the American continent. It was different, voluntary, for economic betterment and opportunity for their children. The Oneidas in New York state were doing well, but most of their tribe had been relocated to Wisconsin. Land trust cases were still in the courts, unresolved after hundreds of years of theft.

The tribal police were cooperative though not overjoyed to see us. Why would they be? It was a constant and genuine complaint that, depending on what political party was in power, the Department of Interior did not always treat Native Americans well. The tribal lands were sovereign and we were interlopers.

Charlie was diplomatic, kind and patient. Once again, I noted his patience. A woman had been killed in New Paltz, an Oneida woman, he began. Her name was Polly Cooper. He didn't mention David's disappearance or the soldiers. The first request he made was simple: "Has Ms. Cooper's family been informed of her death?" They had, the officer told us. And yes, of course, he would provide an escort to her family's home, a young recruit, still a bit green. "They're not very enthusiastic," Peg said as we got back into Charlie's car.

We followed the escort for about an hour, driving west into the sunset. The land was hardscrabble, as eroded as a desert. All the tribe's investment had gone into the casinos and factories. This designated slice of real estate was not the same Mother Earth the tribe had roamed in pre-colonial times, which might explain the alienation and disregard of its inhabitants.

* * *

The house was a trailer in bad repair set on a lonely windswept hill overlooking a small pond. The landscape around the trailer was tranquil, with a 360-degree view of sky and banking clouds, hawks circling in the updrafts, and cows pasturing in the valley below. But the trailer itself was a scene out of a Walker Evans' photo during the Great Depression: worn clothes on a line, half-dressed children, and a woman with long braids in the doorway, the ground underfoot dusty and careworn, as was the woman, who was young. She was Polly Cooper's daughter, Clare. Yes, she'd been informed of her mother's murder. No, she had no idea who might have done it. Her mother's good-for-nothing third husband was long gone, she said. She sounded Irish when she spoke, gesticulating under her apron with calloused hands that rose to her chest as she became animated. Her dry skin hung off her slight frame in folds and her eyes were jaundiced with drink. Her mother had been a hard worker, not a drinker, so what Clare said about her didn't make sense and wasn't reliable. If Polly Cooper had sent money to her daughter it probably had been consumed in drink.

"Do you have a brother?" Peg asked.

"He's a good-for-nothing, too," she said.

Something was going on inside the trailer which sounded like a crashing plate and then a scuffle. Clare Cooper stepped down towards us and called frantically for her three small children. There was a boy and two girls, all under the age of ten, playing with old pots and cooking utensils near the well. Children in all cultures can make a game out of nothing: a sand castle out of dirt and rocks, a tent out of sheets under a table, hop scotch out of shards of shrapnel, hide and seek in bomb craters and burnt out houses. After the American invasion, many buildings in Baghdad were unsafe. We had to stop the children from playing in them, an impossible task. They were everywhere, untended, orphans after an apocalypse. Charlie said, "Let's put the children into one of the vehicles." And then Peg asked, "Who is in the trailer?"

"That's my good-for-nothing brother, Vincent," Clare Cooper said.

He came out in a rush and ran down the hill, the tribal escort in pursuit, long dark hair flying. "That's the shape-shifter from the preserve on the day of the fire," Charlie said.

"And the second soldier in the Popov house," I said.

We waited at the top of the hill, then saw and heard nothing for a long time. One of the children had started crying and calling for her mother. A dog could have done better rounding up its young.

"Is there anything in the trailer for them to eat?" I asked.

In a normal household it was time for supper, a bath, and a story before bedtime.

CHAPTER 13

The tribal escort had the unlikely name of Alfredo. He returned alone, without his prey. He had never given chase before or fired a gun at a suspect, he told us.

Charlie said, "You did fine. He's a shape shifter."

But Alfredo hadn't done fine. He was like a new, enthusiastic recruit sent to war who is both dumb and terrified. Only raw experience would help him figure out how to avoid embarrassing himself on the job.

We let Alfredo talk to Clare Cooper as we stood behind him and listened. Her brother had been in trouble for a long time, she said, and then he'd enlisted in the army, which hadn't straightened him out. Now there was a foul spirit inside him that could not be purged. Even the medicine man could not purge it. No, she didn't know any of his army buddies. No, she had never heard of David Rizzo.

Charlie came forward and asked, "Could he have killed your mother?"

"He did kill our mother," Clare Cooper said.

"How do you know?" Alfredo asked.

"Because he crowed to me about it," she said. "He brought money and food for the children so I let him stay."

Somehow the scene—her brother arriving with food and money—did not sound believable. The children were obviously starving. I reminded myself to ask Alfredo about social services on the reservation. More and more, I was obsessed with saving children: Anwar in Iraq, Fatima and, now, Clare Cooper's children who were what in Trollope and Dickens' time would have been called waifs. I asked if we'd be able to take them away immediately, but Alfredo said that wouldn't be possible; he'd make the necessary calls when he was back in the office.

Meanwhile, Vincent Cooper had escaped and was nowhere to be found. Perhaps it was better, for the moment, Charlie said, as he might lead us to Boris Popov, another man who didn't worry much about honor.

I thought of the uniform we had been asked to wear on behalf of the United States government, what it symbolized. Even a plain uniform without heraldic insignia, badges, and decorations for valor, has meaning for a soldier. Every new soldier asks himself if he can live up to the standard implied. If our commanders look deeply enough into every individual soldier's character, if they are honest about their expectations about a soldier's performance, they know that this initial sense of honor may not be enough to carry their platoons into battle and back into civilian life. There are drunkards in the ranks, criminals, semi-literate vagabonds. They cannot be re-formed as honorable men and women in a mere six weeks at boot camp. And then there are the horrors and distortions of war itself. If we have entered the battle without a foundation of honor to stand on, we will more than likely kill with impunity.

And so it was with Vincent Cooper and others who have become killers in civilian life, or turned inward and taken their own lives.

CHAPTER 14

Charlie Griffith's glass-enclosed office let in a lot of light. But it had its disadvantage: lack of privacy. It was sound-proofed enough, but anyone passing could see the drooping plants on the window sill, the pegs piercing the cork bulletin board, the mug shots of suspects, and the gestures and facial expressions of Charlie and his visitors. Mike Fuller was sitting in a chair near the filing cabinets absorbed in a book when we returned after our pastoral interlude at the reservation. Someone had let him in, or he'd persuaded someone to let him in. Files were everywhere—some open, some closed, others in the filing cabinet. If Mike had wanted a good look, he could have managed it easily. I could see that Charlie was not pleased. He knew Mike Fuller as an honest reporter, but he didn't want him, or anyone else, in his office unattended. "Did my assistant let you in?" he asked.

"Three hours ago. She didn't know when you'd be back. You know I can sweet talk, Charlie. You look good, how's it going?"

"You know Peg Singer and Alison Jenkins?"

"Sure," Mike said. "I'm trying to figure out the FBI's interest in the David Rizzo case. Is there anything you can tell me on or off the record?" he continued.

It was past nine o'clock at night and the office was mostly silent. All I wanted was home, bed, and Trollope. We had traveled in one car and Peg's and mine were in the lot. That was the only reason we'd stopped. We'd de-briefed all the way down and didn't need to talk any more until we'd had a good night's rest.

"What would you like to know?" Charlie asked, throwing the question back at him, a well-honed technique.

Mike got up out of his chair and drifted to the window. A cat cried in the distance. It sounded like a whining baby.

Mike said, "On or off the record, Charlie. Do you want Alison and Peg to leave?"

"They stay," Charlie said. "We're working as a team. Didn't Alison mention that?"

"Yes, she did, of course. But she's working for the family and you are not."

"That's where you're mistaken, Mike. We are all very much working for the family here."

"So where's the FBI in this story?"

"Didn't David answer that question?" I asked. "Didn't you tell me that David had contacted you?"

"He never made it to our rendezvous," Mike said.

He finished his sentence with a strange twisted motion of his shoulders, which in others less lanky would have been a shrug. But in Mike it was tender and forgiving. He wasn't going anywhere until he had some answers or another lead. Like detectives, reporters are persistent. If we didn't tell him what he wanted to know, someone else would.

I waited for Charlie to say more. Our interest, Peg's and mine, was still in David and his parents. We had to protect them even though we had no idea where they were. We couldn't separate the killings from the kidnappings or Agent Dolan's presence.

It was confusing the way Charlie was talking for all of us, using the pronoun "we," in every sentence. And now he did it again. "We are not in Agent Dolan's confidence," Charlie explained, a simple truth which required no embellishment. He had a capacity for directness. Still, it was confusing and my loyalties were divided. I wanted Mike Fuller to get the story and to thank me for it over a candlelight dinner in his cabin. And I wanted more than anything to find David and his parents, dead or alive. Again, I said this to myself: dead or alive. A picture of their deadness continued to haunt me. It was like walking too close to a cliff and, inexplicably, the cliff becomes a magnet drawing the walker over its edge. I'd read about the compulsion to jump, bodies flying downward without a chute. The jump into death feels inevitable; the person does not necessarily have to be suicidal. It's not unlike the risks climbers take every day, or renegade soldiers. And I felt it now, the vertigo, nerve endings raw, my skin pickled with goose bumps, a chill in my spine. If we let go, David and his parents would die and, rationally, of course, that would be more terrible than finding them alive, but it would also be an odd kind of relief after a struggle. The worst would have happened, we would not have to prevent it anymore, so we could let go and fly off the cliff without a chute. I knew I'd have to discuss these dark thoughts with my shrink soon enough. I had no idea what she would say about them, or what I could do about them, but I would, most certainly, have to discuss them.

"So you have nothing to tell me?" Mike asked.

"We can't help you with this one, Mike," Charlie said.

"I am disappointed," Mike said.

"There will be other opportunities for us to share information, as there have been in the past," Charlie said.

"But this is not one of them?"

"Correct," Charlie said. "Thanks for waiting for me, Mike. Hope to see you again soon."

And with that he extended his hand. Mike took it and said, "Secrets, even innocent secrets, are always an incitement to a reporter, Charlie. I'd like you to be part of this story. Or the three of you can be anonymous sources, deep background. Would that be okay?"

"That won't work in this situation," Charlie said, firmly.

Peg had been silent the whole time. Now she just said she'd be on her way and then hesitated as she put on her coat as though a thought had slipped through her memory and she was trying to retrieve it. Her voice lifted into a higher register as she said, "We'll stay in touch, Mike. If it's possible to talk, we'll give you a call."

Did she wink at Mike? It was the first time it occurred to me that Charlie had silenced us and that he might be acting on Agent Dolan's instructions to keep us muzzled.

* * *

It had been a long, over-stimulating day and I had trouble getting to sleep. Finally, at 3 a.m. I called Mike assuming that if he didn't want to answer his phone, it would be off, and I could leave him a message. I wasn't sure what I wanted to say because I thought he, too, had caught Charlie's use of the pronoun "we" and that he had something to say he had then decided not to say. I suppose I knew him well enough to catch concern in his expression. He picked up on one ring and offered to come over before I'd even finished my sentence. It felt as though he'd been waiting by the phone until the sun came up so he could call me and that we'd both been sleepless for the same reason. It wasn't until after we became lovers that we admitted we were tuned in to each other in this way. But that day, I had no thoughts of making love. I was too exhausted and preoccupied with the case.

It took him an hour to drive over. By then, I had fallen asleep over my book. I let him in and went back into the bedroom to change out of my nightgown. The weather had warmed and it was almost summer. I had yet to get out all my summer clothes. I threw on a pair of too-thick jeans and was sorry for it as soon as I sat down. It became an unwanted distraction, almost a fixation, as we spoke.

Mike put up the kettle and offered me breakfast in my own kitchen. I liked the way he made himself at home and felt at home anywhere. I had noticed that in Iraq, how he slid in with both the Americans and the Iraqis. He spoke Arabic, among other languages.

"There is something more I wanted to tell you, Alison," he said. "I do have news of David. I am glad you called because I realized as soon as I drove away from New Paltz that I cannot withhold this information from you."

"Where is he?"

"In Pennsylvania. He's at a motel with his parents under an assumed name. I'll give you the phone number. He's waiting to hear from you."

"So he kidnapped his parents?"

"He rescued them," Mike said.

CHAPTER 15

P eg said that it was no good thinking I could save David and his parents by myself without her help, that wasn't the way to proceed. I was too tired and too slow to argue with her. She was still playing supervisor, keeping such a close rein on me that I couldn't think. I was sorry I had told her about Mike's visit. On the other hand, she was impressed that he had come to see me, that we had met in Iraq. But I had a ways to go before she cut me loose, which I assumed she would do as soon as this case was solved or closed. She had described the difference between closure and resolution to Agent Dolan. I'd never heard anything so humble on the subject before.

My telephone rang almost as soon as I was off the phone with her. She had more to say, but it would have to be in person she had said as we were signing off. And so I knew then that our phones were tapped and was relieved I hadn't revealed too many details of my discussion with Mike Fuller, only that he'd been to see me, that it would be a very hot day, that David and his parents were alive somewhere and would she like to come over for lunch. "I'm on my way," she said.

The emptiness in my house suddenly felt excruciating. Peg lived only a half-hour away and it was a long half-hour. I went out onto my deck, but the sun at mid-morning was already searing.

My edible potted plants—tomatoes, herbs, lettuce—were wilting. I got out my watering can, soaked them, and trimmed off the dead leaves. I hadn't been paying attention to much of anything recently. How would I ever care for a cat, or children, or a significant other?

Peg arrived and her reassuring presence steadied me. I was just a war-torn kid and needed her more than I was willing to admit.

We agreed that Charlie was out of the loop for the time being until we knew for certain that he wasn't working for the FBI or under their thumb. And then Peg said, "I want you to go to Pennsylvania. I'll tell Charlie you need a few days of R &R. Go to the motel, call into my cell VM only and leave coded messages. I'll try to figure something out and, eventually, I'll talk to Charlie. I've known him for a long time."

The scorching sun drenched the deck and Peg's face. She smiled whenever she spoke of Charlie. She loved Charlie and wanted to believe in him, she told me. How had she loved him? I wasn't sure and didn't want to ask. The small patch of wood on which she stood seemed like the edge of my own future. I could step in either direction—forwards or backwards. Peg was giving me the choice and choice always demands courage. Was I prepared to travel to Pennsylvania on my own? she asked. Yes, I said, definitely yes. "Drive down to Newburgh and rent a car. Make sure you are not being followed."

* * *

The motel was in Chadds Ford, Pennsylvania, home to the Wyeth Museum which I had always wanted to visit. David met me there and we sketched on a bench overlooking the Delaware River. Students from a local college had rented canoes and were having a raucous time steering clear of rocks and pylons. I couldn't remember the last time I'd had fun and wanted to get into a canoe with them. But David was sitting next to me. He was cleaned up, wearing jeans and a T-shirt, his soldier- self undercover. "My parents are scared," he said. "I need to get them somewhere secure."

"Peg's working on that," I said. "Will you go with them?"

"I am not sure," he said. "I must finish what I have started. The Popovs are killers. They already think my parents know too much."

His voice was soft and far away, talking to me across a vast distance, his words as fragile as the air bubbles on the river. He had abandoned his combat boots and camouflage, his face was clean shaven, his hair shiny. He had once been a boy about to go to war. He had not come home, not even now, and there was not much left to interest him except for what it was he had to finish, he said.

"I assume you have told Mike Fuller what you have to finish?" I said.

"Mike knows," David says. "He has stored electronic files and informed his editors where they are located."

"So this is a big story?"

"Yes, Alison."

"And the documents you had hidden in your parents' house?"

"All with Mike," he said.

"So I suppose our job is done here, Peg's and mine. We have found you and you have been reunited with your parents."

But he did not answer my rhetorical question. He put his hand on mine and we sat by the river side by side for a while longer. Then we went inside the museum and took a tour with Andrew Wyeth's grand-daughter, Victoria. It was obvious that she loved her grand-father very much and knew his work intimately. David was touched by her devotion to the family and the family's story, both tragic and joyous: a violent death of a grandson at a rail crossing, Andrew Wyeth driving the car, and then a clandestine love affair documented in a series of paintings only recently discovered. The family was shattered, but carried on, David said.

I ate dinner that night with the Rizzos in a non-descript pizza restaurant in town, a few moments of freedom in their now fugitive life. We agreed that they should stay in the motel until Peg contacted them with concrete plans. I could not stay with them because my absence would be noticed eventually, Peg said. She and Mike were organizing an escort to Canada. The escort would be arriving in a day or two. The Rizzos had become refugees, but for what reason? What were they running from exactly?

I said goodbye matter-of-factly. It was a trick I'd learned in the army, almost a superstition, to be laid-back before departure to the front, or from the front back to base, and then home. We make light of good-byes in a war-time army. We never know if we will see each other again.

* * *

New York has sixty-two counties. Each county is divided into towns, townships, incorporated villages or hamlets. The villages have governing bodies, but the hamlets don't. There are village boards, mayors, town supervisors, boards of supervisors. It's very baffling especially when law enforcement has to decide jurisdiction. When Fatima's body washed up on the banks of the Hudson, the remnants of her body were in Columbia County. But her brown skirt was found in Rensselaer County and her shirt and head scarf further south in Greene County. These were my obsessive thoughts as I drove top speed out of Pennsylvania, through New Jersey, onto the Palisades—one of my favorites, old truck-free parkways—and then the New York State Thruway, until I arrived at Exit 18 in New Paltz. Incomprehension gnawed at me en route, vacancy, impotence. I collapsed into the softest chair in

Charlie's office where Charlie, Peg and Agent Dolan were waiting for me. All questions about jurisdiction evaporate in the presence of the FBI, but they make mistakes and we cannot allow them to be right when they are not right, I thought. If I lied now about where I had been for two days, so be it, I would be taking a risk. I did not care. I had to know that David and his parents were in Canada and, even then, what would I say about them?

"It is always the same when things go wrong," Agent Dolan said. "We blame ourselves. Our loyalties become confused."

It was not sympathy or concern I heard in her voice; she was scolding me. Where had I been?

I reiterated the cover story about R&R but I did not say where I had been. I had to remind myself that Agent Dolan had learned to lie with impunity and her agents may have been following me all along. I looked out the window down to the Wallkill River which was running high after a torrential rain. A canoe swiveled around and headed back upstream. I could hear laughter, workers picking debris out of the polluted river.

"A couple of days of R&R?" she asked yet again.

"Yes," I said.

The image of David next to me on the bench by the river remained with me until Agent Dolan left. I was by his side, his buddy in the trenches, and there wasn't anything I wouldn't do to protect him. Agent Dolan was wrong about me; my loyalties were strong.

* * *

Another hot August day, nearing the end of summer. The blackberries along the roadside were covered with dust. A call came in from Charlie: Mrs. Popov had been picked up by the paramedics on Main Street in Redhook. She had landed chest first on the sidewalk in front of a new upscale Thai restaurant. The owner had given her a glass of water and then called 911. Charlie heard the call on the radio and rushed over. After the paramedics cleared her, he put her into the back seat of his patrol car.

"I'm on my way," he told Peg.

"On your way where?"

"Your place," he said.

Peg didn't object because David had disappeared again and we were back on the case. His parents had arrived in Canada without him.

* * *

It was the first time I had a chance to observe Mrs. Popov without the distraction of men with guns: her son, Boris, her husband, Vladimir, Vincent Cooper. The second soldier in the house that day was Vincent Cooper. In the most uncomplicated of explanations, Mrs. Popov was less a spouse than a cook and nanny, a victim, sucked into the vortex of a small army of miscreants. I remember how she had tried to stop her husband from hurting me, how she had said something to Boris, how Boris and Vladimir had both told her to shut up.

She was a peasant woman dressed in cheap clothes. Her features were delicate but her body was robust. Her eyes were dry, melancholy, and so deeply set she almost looked blind. She was talking rapidly in Russian with a smattering of English, the words spilling into each other. "Please, please," was obvious enough. She was in a daze, tired and overheated.

Peg took her to the spare bedroom, pulled out a towel and wash cloth, put a glass of cool water on the bedside table. Mrs. Popov sat down slowly, sinking into the bed, her shoulders slipping onto her bruised chest. She had a strange odor: part sweat, part loamy earth, not unpleasant. "Please, please," she said again and then, "Thank you." She lay down quietly and we stood there, the three of us, watching her as she fell asleep. She must have been walking all day, Charlie said. The soles of her shoes were nearly gone.

"We'll have some explaining to do to the FBI," Charlie said.

"I'll leave that to you, Charlie," Peg said.

Sooner or later, we are tested, I thought. We might think we are obligated to obey, to hold secrets, to support corrupt politicians, our husbands, our lovers. But then the day comes and we do the right thing. Mrs. Popov had done the right thing.

CHAPTER 16

It was a quiet morning, no wind stirring, cars in the distance. Even in the depths of the country, solitude is an illusion in our built-up world. Irena Popov was propped on her left elbow when I went back in the room at first light to see how she was doing. Eight hours had passed, Charlie had gone home, but I had stayed the night on Peg's pull-out couch in the living room. I slept soundly, more soundly than I had in many weeks. Was it possible I was having fun? Enjoying a sense of camaraderie and purpose? The communal life of the army had suited me, an antidote to the claustrophobia of a nuclear family. And I was pleased that we had Irena Popov, thanks to Charlie. His instinct was to defy the FBI and to sequester this sad and exhausted woman. There was a lot to think about, he said. If we handed her over, she could be sent overseas to an interrogation center administered by a despotic regime, a sweet new twist known as rendition.

Before my stint in the army, I had not thought of anything beyond my most immediate concerns. I didn't even vote. But I'd changed a lot. Now, as a civilian, I was drawn to disturbances and had decided to become a private investigator to resolve them. "So as a PI, am I correct, you have a license to kill?" my therapist asked me one day. "Is that what you mean by resolve?"

What had I said to prompt this question? Oh yes, I wanted to blow the Popovs and Vincent Cooper away—far away—with a high-powered rifle. Had I said this out loud? And I wanted to save David. I was determined to save David. He was a comrade in arms, a soldier. After delivering his parents to relatives in Canada, he had returned and called to say he was back, his parents were okay. Then he had vanished again.

I walked back into the bedroom. "Breakfast is on the table," I said. I'd scrambled up some eggs which, oddly, clarified my thinking.

* * *

The trip down to Vassar to search for a translator took about forty-five minutes. I passed the Rizzo's abandoned house on the way. I wondered when the oil would run out and when the well-tended garden would become wilderness. Left alone, nature invades man-made shelter quickly. The flying squirrels, the chipmunks, mice, even rat snakes, find their way inside; houses collapse into the forest and become one with it. Further along: the FDR estate and the trailer park. I kept my foot on the accelerator and kept my eyes on the road.

I found a translator within an hour: Svetlana, Lana for short. She was twenty-years-old, more than willing, and she needed the money. It would be something to record in her memoirs, she said, with the self-confidence I'd noticed in the few young Russian women I'd met. I had a soldier friend who lived in Brighton Beach and she had invited me from time to time to swim in the ocean there and hang out in restaurants and clubs. I liked the Russians, sly as they sometimes are, a legacy of growing up in an oppressive communist regime. Lana was younger than the generation I knew, but she was just as self-sure and dramatic.

Carol Bergman

So we set out, the five of us, about noon on a very hot and humid mid-summer day, in Charlie's unmarked SUV owned by the State of New York, an irony of sorts. And I had no idea where we were going exactly, nor did Peg, it seemed, until we were well underway and headed onto the Northway towards Canada. We stopped at a mall and found a Friendly's and it was there, in the most banal of locations, that we deposed Irena Popov using a digital tape recorder, a notebook computer and two moleskins— Peg's and mine—for backup before we sent off the translated transcripts to Mike Fuller:

My name is Irena Popov. My husband is Vladimir, my son is Boris. I also have another son, Andre. He is a doctor living in California, thank God he is away from here with his wife and my two grandchildren. Vladimir and Boris both are working for the American government, I hope you believe me. You will check on this, yes? I do not lie.

I am a mother. I am a wife. But when my son and my husband returned one night with blood on their hands and fire in their eyes, I knew they had done a very bad thing, much more than ever before, even in Iraq or Afghanistan so many years ago. Please God I do not know what they did there. How could it be worse than this? Boris was boasting to his father about the girl.

(voice of Private Investigator Margaret Singer) What girl, Mrs. Popov?

The American girl. The one who was in love with David.

(voice of M.S.) Go on.

They gave her drugs. They raped her. They forced David to watch. They said to him, let this be a warning. You will say nothing about what we are doing. Do you understand? Nothing. Then when they came back to the house, they forced him to have sex with the girl.

(voice of M.S.) Which girl are we talking about now, Mrs. Popov?

The little girl, Fatima.

(voice of M.S.) Who killed her, Mrs. Popov?

Boris, he put David's hand on the gun, but he pulled the trigger. David, he was in the house when this woman was there (pointing to

Private Investigator Alison Jenkins) but he was hiding in the back room. He was trying to save the girl and more girls before.

(voice of M.S.) Were you there? Did you witness this shooting?

Yes.

(voice of M.S.) Where are they now—Boris, Vladimir and Vincent?

I don't know.

(voice of M.S.) And David Rizzo?

That boy. That boy how he tried to stop the killing. They beat him. And they said they would harm his parents. We know this is true, that they can do this, that they can do anything and no one will stop them.

The translator said there might be a problem with tense. She did her best, she said, it was accurate to the best of her ability, but Irena Popov was not an educated woman and even in Russian, there were confusions. "Working," continuous present tense, might be "have worked," in the not so distant past. They might have worked for the American government. Or, they might still be working for the American government.

Agent Dolan called on Charlie's cell. "I can triangulate, you know that, Charlie. I hope you want to keep your job. Just tell me exactly where you are and we'll come to get Mrs. Popov and that will be the end of it, Charlie." We could hear shots busting out of his blue tooth which he pulled off his ear. "She called from the shooting range," he said. Then he turned off the GPS. "Funny that the GPS should slip my mind. I don't usually have to run away from anything." Nobody spoke for a while after that, we just sat in silence, the car rocking gently along the smooth road, windows shut and the air conditioner at comfort level, night falling deep and slow as we continued driving north.

So there we were, approaching Canada, our friendly neighbor to the north, in an unmarked New York State SUV, a State employee at the wheel, without clout, without exit or entry papers for Irena Popov. And we all looked tired and disheveled after the long journey. Huddled together in the car, traveling without suitcases or possessions, we had bonded, as humans always do in small spaces; we might have been a family seeking asylum from a war zone. When the United States immigration officer asked to see our papers, Charlie stepped out of the car and went into the booth and we sat and waited. I offered grapes, energy bars, water. My nurturing instinct was strong, we were all sheltered in the vehicle together and it was a solid, typical, all-American vehicle in the less than solid, typical, American side of the border. How had David Rizzo negotiated this passage—out of one country and into another—for his frightened parents? Life turns on a dime, I thought. Diana and Mel Rizzo had become IDPs, internally displaced people, and traveling across a border, they had become refugees. Hopefully, it wouldn't be forever and the end of their story would be peaceful, a return to the predictable world of a small town and all its implied securities, where justice is always done.

Charlie returned to the car and said, "There's a stop order. Our names have been flagged in the computer as fugitives."

"In any other country, we could present a bribe," I said, only half joking. Then the officer came out of the booth and escorted all of us into a small cinder block building, spacious inside, computer central. "At least we haven't been tagged as suspected terrorists," Peg said. Both of us were in a wry mood but Lana was agitated. She was worried about her student visa and wanted to make it clear that she wasn't leaving the United States. "None of us are," Charlie continued calmly, "except this woman, Irena Popov. She is a material witness in an important case we are working on and is in grave danger. I want to arrange protective custody for her in

Canada." He spoke slowly, respectfully. There is no need to hurry, I thought.

The officer excused himself and walked towards the Canadian side. He was weary, Charlie commented, at the end of his shift. "Not a man in love with his own authority," Charlie said as we watched him disappear across No Man's Land into another cinder block building. He was smiling when he returned, friendly, his role as stern gatekeeper had changed and I noticed his eyes for the first time—green—and the crow's feet at their edges. His mouth was thin, framed by a bushy white mustache. He was not only weary but near retirement, more philosophical perhaps, more flexible. He had persuaded the Canadians to take Irena Popov into protective custody. "I never saw those stop orders," he said, pleased with himself, I think, that he had the courage to ignore orders. But then Irena wouldn't go with him and Lana had to talk to her gently in Russian until she understood that she'd be safe in Canada. "We will contact your son, Andre," Peg said. I gave Irena what was left of the food and water we had bought en route. I was anxious for her and eager for her son, Andre—the good son, the doctor—to be with his mother.

CHAPER 17

On the way down from Canada, we stopped at a motel to get some sleep and then we drove to the reservation. Vincent Cooper was still at large and this was not good news. There was no way for the tribal police to ignore the importance of capturing him and, once found, they'd have to turn him over to Charlie Griffith for extradition.

Vincent Cooper was a desperate man, a violent man, and he was armed; he had been in the United States Army where he had been taught to use state-of-the-art weapons. They had found a cache in the corn field behind his sister's house.

Before Vincent Cooper had signed up, his family and everybody who knew him thought him mad and stayed clear. In the old days, he might have been a shaman, a man possessed, a man with second sight. But the spirits inside him had turned evil, fueled by drugs, alcohol and guns.

* * *

My therapist had asked if I was doing anything for fun, if my life was in balance, so I told her about the hummingbirds.

"The hummingbirds?"

"Yes," I said. "They are slight as a dragonfly. I can watch them for hours jumping from branch to branch, nectar spilling onto the ground from the feeder. First the male with its iridescent green back, white underbelly and white-tipped tail. Then the brown-feathered female, subdued in color but vibrant all the same."

"I see," she said. "And they make you feel, how, exactly?"

"They lift my spirits," I said.

But when I arrived home, the hummingbird feeder was on the deck, nectar everywhere, probably a black bear or the squirrels again, and now a feast for the yellow jackets. I left the feeder where it was and went back inside to get something to eat. I had taken out insurance on my future and started researching a new case. I wanted to get back to it. If it worked out, I'd ask Peg if I could partner with her again. A wind energy company was harassing homeowners, trying to buy them out, and setting fires on their land. This would be a simpler case, I thought, without the FBI breathing on us. So I made phone calls and started a new notebook where I recorded basic information. But I couldn't figure out who would pay our fee. The homeowners were poor homesteaders living in trailers and shacks on the edge of a stream at the bottom of a mountain the wind company wanted. One or two didn't have running water or electricity. The land abutted State Forest and a maze of challenging hiking trails. The State Department of Environmental Protection had also stated their objections to the private company building wind turbines anywhere nearby. Then the fires had started and the town meetings. The struggle was volatile but there hadn't been any random killings or threats. I needed a break from threats. So I went out there—it wasn't far from the southern edge of the Ashokan reservoir—to take a look, ask some questions—and in the midst of a conversation with an old man whose grandfather had once lived in one of the buried towns under the reservoir, a couple of hikers walked by and, when I greeted them, they looked frightened and said they were headed to their car and did the old man have a phone because there was a man in a lean-to at the top of one of the trails and they didn't like the look of him. I told the hikers to follow me out of the dense, dark valley and back onto Rte. 28. We were very near the Popov's farm. The hikers took off at high speed. I called Peg and then Charlie on the two-way radio. I felt as though I was back where I had started though I had, at least, taken down the hikers' names and phone numbers and called for back-up. I wasn't planning on going into that house alone again, or so I thought.

When the troopers finally arrived—and the wait seemed endless—they told me to stay in my car which I had parked across the road in Helga Schmidt's driveway. She offered me a chair in the kitchen and a bag of tomatoes to take home. She seemed glad of my company though she wasn't talkative. Limited conversation was a characteristic of some of the farmers I'd met, men and women of few words, embedded in a landscape of storm-felled trees, lichen-covered rocks and cultivated gardens. I wondered what the years ahead would be like for all of us if wind companies and more cell towers came in.

When the troopers arrived, I went across the road, sat on a rock at the far end of the dirt parking area, and waited. Only Vladimir Popov was inside, the troopers said. What's he doing in there?" I asked. "Tapping away on his computer," the trooper said.

"What about the barn?"

"We'd need a search warrant."

I was sure the barn had already been searched or emptied and that Vladimir was protecting, feeding and instructing his son, Boris, who was hiding out in the mountains. I couldn't decide if I should talk to Vladimir Popov or not, what good it would do, what difference it would make, or if I'd ever see David Rizzo again. But then the troopers left and five minutes later I was inside the house talking to Vladimir Popov. "Does Agent Dolan know you are here?" he asked. He was even smiling a little. I regarded this peaceful expression as the resentment on a condemned man's face. But I was wrong. He was probably dreaming of his retirement in the Russian countryside or his bank account. How could we stop his escape? I was talking as though I had authority. I had no authority. He was not worried about Irena, he said, when I told him she was in protective custody. "She will not sing," he said. "She will be finished soon in any case. The American government will not let you touch me." And then he turned back to his computer and wished me a good evening.

* * *

We decided to go after Boris Popov anyway. His father may have been involved in espionage, but the son was a cold-blooded killer on our turf, taking advantage of the cover his father provided. "Let the FBI try to stop us now," Charlie said. He'd had enough.

* * *

Gunshots ahead and guinea fowl scattering led us to the camp site. We hid behind boulders of schist. Eventually, Boris Popov ran out of ammunition and the firing stopped. He had clambered to the summit and we could see his shadow and then his body, hands in the air. He had tied a white T-shirt to the barrel of his gun. But the surrender was a false ending as he scurried up the hill and vanished into the night.

"Is there any way we can call Vladimir Popov in for questioning without Agent Dolan present?" I asked. "He threatened to kill his wife. He's either the kingpin or an accomplice. I'm sure Boris is visiting the house at regular intervals. Can we stake it out?"

"The FBI is telling me to leave it alone," Charlie said.

I couldn't read his tone. Had he finally succumbed to the pressure?

"For God's sake, Charlie, there have been three murders," Peg said. "We can't spin our wheels on their account. We have to believe in something."

And I realized then how much Peg had felt stymied by the presence of the FBI. She was trying to transmit her concern forcefully. I had never seen her lose it, not for a second, since I had started working for her. She had served the Rizzos faithfully and to what end? They were in Canada without their son who had returned to finish what he had deemed unfinished, yet he was still missing, living undercover somewhere. "The trouble is we have lost our power to know what is real and what is false," Peg said. "This is what that Patriot Act has done to us. We've all become suspects."

Charlie said, "I'll pull Vladimir Popov in for questioning. I assume you'll both want to be there."

"It is too late to change my profession," Peg said, and for a moment I thought she meant it, not that it was too late, but that she might consider changing her profession.

* * *

After we made love, I slept with my back to the wall facing him. He had left the night light on for me so I would not stumble if I needed to go to the bathroom. In the morning, he turned over and embraced me and wanted to make love again, but I pushed him away, got up and stood by the window. It was a Sunday, more than ten months since David Rizzo had first disappeared. Across the street, next to the Five and Dime, an old woman carrying two plastic bags struggled with the lid of a dumpster. White hair, hands wrinkled like old leaves, she walked away down Main Street towards the train station. Sergeant Ed De Beyer came up behind me and said, "Is there anyone you won't help?" His admiration embarrassed me and though the sex had been pleasant enough, I didn't want to be there anymore. I was with the wrong man and both of us knew it. "I was never able to bring a woman home," he said. He had been eager to tell me about his prominent, liberal Old Dutch family, which nonetheless had restricted him in many ways. His father was a judge and had wanted Ed to go to law school. "So of course he is disappointed in me," Ed said. He looked like a schoolboy. I had outgrown schoolboys long ago.

That night, I played a game of darts at Jane's with Charlie, Rosie and Peg. Ed walked in and Charlie said to me, "Did you know that kid's father is a judge? Old Dutch family related to the Beekmans—sheriffs and judges, going back to colonial times."

"That explains his manners," Peg said. "He was born to them."

The place was half-filled with locals, a few hikers and climbers. Charlie invited Ed to join us and Ed agreed. I greeted him as though he were a stranger. Rosie picked up where Charlie had left off, welcoming Ed and asking him questions about his family. I wasn't planning to tell her I'd slept with him. She had fastened her eyes on Ed and kept them there for a long time like he was a passage in a book she was reading and didn't understand. Her lips moved a little. She might have been praying that Ed would notice her, take her out, and take her to bed. This would have been okay with me, but Ed wasn't interested in Rosie, he was hooked on me. I excused myself and said I had to get home, I was tired, it had been a long day. I had no confidence that my impolite departure would sit well with Rosie. Eventually I'd have to explain to her that I'd slept with Ed and that I felt bad about it, not for me, but for him. It was my habit, it seemed, to get into knots with men, knots of my own making. My therapist thought I enjoyed hurting men otherwise why would I reel them in and toss them away like confetti. I had never before felt the discomfort of responsibility but

I felt it now and it hurt, which I suppose was a good thing. I had to try not to be so careless in the future and apologize to Ed when I had a chance, I decided. His birthday was coming up he had told me. I could invite him to dinner. But I didn't get to think about Ed during the following week because I was busy on the Rizzo case again. We had been paid, Peg and I, to find him and he was missing again. He had traveled to Canada with his parents and, so far as we knew, he had returned to the United States. He had called to tell me he was back, but the call could have been from anywhere and he might have lied. He was still at large, as was Vincent Cooper and Boris Popov. So I was pleased when Charlie called to say that Vladimir Popov was in his office, how soon could we come over? "And Agent Dolan?" I asked. "She's down in Newburgh. The FBI has set up a new office there." Charlie was not necessarily a man of vision, but he was a good man, and he had called Vladimir Popov in for questioning without telling Agent Pat Dolan.

* * *

Vladimir Popov's shoulders were stooped, his round spectacles askew on his face. Charlie began with a polite introduction. He explained that the matter was serious, there'd been three murders and a young, possibly drugged, possibly kidnapped foreign girl had been seen in his house. Burlap bags with the logo of the farm had been appearing throughout the county. They were filled with bones. His wife, Irena, was safe and comfortable.

"We will all be asking you questions and recording your answers," Charlie said. "When you are completely de-briefed, we'll allow you to call your attorney. Is that clear?"

No answer.

"Is that clear, Mr. Popov? Do you understand why you are here?"

"Jenkins, I have met before. Where is Agent Dolan? Am I arrested? Do you think you have the right to arrest me, to question me? If you do, you are mistaken, my friend. You have not read me my Miranda rights."

Charlie said, "Where is your son now, Mr. Popov?"

This was a dead-end line of questioning. We were amateurs compared to Popov and Dolan, he had been right about that. He would not tell us anything or turn state's evidence. Only his wife, Irena, could do that, if she stayed alive, and David Rizzo, if he was still alive. I doubted if Vladimir Popov cared about David Rizzo though his son, Boris, might have spared David's life because he was a battlefield comrade. The ties that bind on the battlefield are strong. Still, I was certain that David was ready to turn them all in and had told Mike Fuller all he needed to know for a series of investigative articles. But I was not prepared for the deaths that might follow our failure to capture Boris Popov and Vincent Cooper. I was certain that the killing had not come to an end and that David Rizzo was still trying to end it.

"You have a complicated conscience," Charlie said to Vladimir Popov. "Or none at all," Peg added.

"The bad child receives just as many sweets," Popov said, as elusive a statement as he made about his wife when I told him she was in protective custody. "She will be finished soon in any case," he had said.

"Is your wife involved in the child slavery ring?" I asked.

"She is a peasant," Vladimir Popov said.

The girl on the floor in the long, brown skirt did not fit into the picture unless she was a slave. I had never discussed a slavery ring, or gun running, or drugs at any length with Peg or Charlie. Our discussions had not been specific to that extent. Whatever racket these men were involved in, they were all equally venal and useful to governments at war, including our own. To get close to the Taliban, we support the opium trade in Afghanistan. We expect illiterate farmers to swing to our side in the same way we assumed

Vladimir Popov would change to our side if the lure was strong enough. But once there is blood and money, there is no loyalty. And it doesn't matter which government pays.

Vladimir Popov said, "There is nothing you can do to keep me here."

"Popov, you do not know what you are saying," I said, though I knew he did. I had been an eyewitness in his house and would testify to what I had seen there, if there ever was a trial. Popov assumed, probably correctly, that there would never be a trial.

It had started to rain hard and I could not see my car as I walked out of the station into the parking lot. The wind came in a sudden blast as I opened the car door and the rain beat on the metal roof and punctuated the radio announcer's words. I turned up the volume: a soldier had been picked up near Woodstock. He had amnesia, didn't know who he was, and had been taken to the VA hospital in Poughkeepsie. Why hadn't Charlie Griffith been informed? Lightening lit the interior of the car. Peg came running out, her jacket over her head, but she didn't stop to talk. And then Vladimir Popov. I rolled down my window and shouted after him, "You no longer have any hope of escape," but this was an empty threat and my words were drowned out by the pelting rain and the high wind. I called Charlie from my cell, but his phone didn't pick up. "Charlie, I'm going down to the VA hospital in Poughkeepsie to check out the soldier." And then I called Peg; she was gone, already out of range. I had to keep moving though I knew I shouldn't go down to the hospital on my own. I could only hope that Charlie and Peg would pick up my messages and meet me there. If the FBI had been asking questions on the reservation, they might be there also. And that would be hard for me.

* * *

The VA out-patient clinics are bursting with injured and disaffected soldiers, the walking wounded. Many have survived roadside bombs and suicide bombers. Is it a mercy to rush highly trained medics onto the battlefield to keep so many soldiers barely alive for the rest of their lives, many of them unable to speak, move or think? And what about the tens of hundreds of thousands of civilians in war zones? What about them? It was an odd thing, but since the flight to Canada with Irena Popov, I had passed into a region of loss and disbelief. I did not think that war did anyone any good or that any new president would be able to end war. Lives turned upside down, villages demolished, permanent, disabling injuries, wounded warriors and maimed children.

The receptionist said that I had no right to make any inquiries. I was a stranger, not a relative. The storm intensified, the lights flickered, and then went on again. In the silence between the thunderclaps, I had taken out my ID; the receptionist was unimpressed. "And I am a veteran," I said, "on a murder case." This softened him and he called for his supervisor who led me down a series of hallways. A pail overturned and clattered on the gray linoleum floor. And a nurse said, "This way, doctor," to a young doctor in civilian clothes. He may have been visiting a relative or he may have been a specialist. We turned down another hallway and then into a room. Vincent Cooper was strapped down on a bed. "He's been sedated," the nurse told me. "I know who he is," I told the supervisor. "I'll put a call in to the State Police. They'll want to put a guard on the door until he comes to and then take him into custody. He's wanted for murder." I asked if they'd keep him tied down until the police arrived and the supervisor said they would, certainly they would. And he looked worried because he must have known that Vincent Cooper would be a danger to all of them once he woke up and realized where he was. A strange sound like footfalls on a pebbled beach came from Vincent Cooper's clenched mouth. The nurse said, "He's gone mad."

Whether he was mad or not is immaterial to me, I thought. I waited for the police detail to arrive and then I left.

* * *

It was Ed's father, Judge Stephen De Beyer, who sent the young soldier to Charlie's office just two days later. He was an amputee, but otherwise intact. He used his prosthetic arms well; he could even drive a car designed especially for robotic limbs. The way back into civilian life was steep, he said. He began to sweat as he talked about Boris Popov and was dismayed to hear he was at large. "Oh please, not here," he said. He was related to the De Beyer's and when he'd heard about David Rizzo's disappearance and the killings, he'd contacted the judge and told him what he knew about Boris Popov's smuggling schemes—young girls, drugs—and the soldiers he had killed during battle after they had threatened to turn him in.

"What about David Rizzo," I asked. "What about him?"

"A true American hero," the soldier said.

"Would you be willing to testify to what you saw and heard ?" I asked. But he would not answer my question. He had taken a long time to find the courage to come forward at all. What would it take to get him to stand up in court and identify Boris Popov as a killer?

CHAPTER 18

I t was a Tuesday night, one of the slowest of the week at the Beekman Arms in Rhinebeck. Summer's end, it was already nearly dark at 7 p.m., autumn in the air. We sat in front of the cold fireplace for a while. Ed ordered a beer, I had a cranberry juice and soda. Then we moved into the conservatory dining room where the windows were open to a small front garden, fragrant mums just starting to bloom. Cars moved slowly through the four-way intersection, a few tourists ambled. I let my mind drift away from Ed and what I wanted to say to him. It wouldn't be the first conversation I ever had with a man I had carelessly slept with. Ed hadn't done anything wrong and I felt terrible. He was younger by three years, younger in experience, a boy, as I had recognized the first time we were together. Was it the war that had made me an old soul, or had my decision to go to war set me apart? The solidity of Ed's family, their deep roots in New York, had cloistered him from many of the demands of modern life. Beyond his desire to give back by becoming a police officer, he carried an anachronistic sense of entitlement which spilled over onto me. Now that he'd made love to me, I must be his. Though it was his birthday, he had brought me a present, a small box wrapped in silver paper. I dreaded opening it. I had nothing for him other than an invitation to dinner. How could I tell him I didn't want to be his girl?

The street lights went on and the cars continued to roll through the intersection. We ordered our meal and I got up to close the window. My thin sweater felt inadequate in the dusky chill. Ed's voice came to me in a fog of patter. I let him talk and didn't interrupt him. The silver package lay unopened near my water glass. I had mumbled that I'd keep it for dessert, but had no idea what I would do when it arrived. It was Ed's birthday dinner. I'd ordered a slice of cake with a candle, singing waiters. In the excitement, maybe Ed would forget that he'd given me a present. A sweet man, I thought. Anything I say will be inadequate.

The dessert came, the singing waiters, Ed blew out the candle set in a delicate crystal holder on the tray, and then he asked me to open the present. It was a long gold necklace with a locket, a picture of Ed inside. "It belonged to my grandmother," he said.

A car went by and lit up the window. I pulled my sweater tighter around my shoulders, took up a spoon and played with the warm chocolate cake on my plate. It was running everywhere.

The end of the meal, the arrival of the check, soft words as I pushed the red velvet box across the table to Ed's side, all took place in slow motion and was mingled with the sounds coming from the street—sirens, police, the hysterical shouts of the other guests in the conservatory as the glass shattered. A door opened and three troopers ordered everyone to evacuate to the parking lot behind the inn. We were shoved into a small barn on the far side where we were told to get onto the ground. Ed identified himself and said he'd like to help and, though he was off duty, in plain clothes, he was given the authority to make certain no one left the barn until an all-clear. There were about twenty of us including an old woman celebrating her 90th birthday. She rested in her daughter's lap and fell asleep. When she woke up a few minutes later, she didn't know where she was. A few words from her son-in-law and she was calm again. For the most part, people do well in a crisis, I thought. It is not just that we help one another but that our survival instincts are strong. If it is best to remain quiet, we will remain quiet. All bodily functions shut down—the desire to eat, to sneeze, to go to the bathroom. And so we shivered on the wet dirt floor for more than two hours. It was remarkable how no one complained and how I only noticed the dirt floor as the troopers stepped inside to release us. They didn't say anything about what had happened, but when we got back onto the street and saw the police dogs, the yellow tape, and a burned-out car close to mine, it was obvious. Though the bomb had been more incendiary than explosive, it was a miracle no one had been hurt.

* * *

Mike Fuller called me from Istanbul to find out if I was alright. He'd seen the news on CNN and I was in one of the panned street shots standing next to Ed De Beyer. The expression on my face told the story: I was scared. Charlie Griffith had told him the rest. "I didn't even know you were in Turkey," I said.

"Watch your back, Alison, we're getting close."

"Close to what?"

"We'll talk in person. Watch your back. No risks."

He didn't say what he was doing in Turkey. I didn't ask. But why did he assume the bomb had been intended for me? "Didn't you say the car bomb was close to your car?"

"I did."

"Well, Alison."

"Well what?"

"Alison..."

The next day I met Peg at Charlie's office for a more thorough de-briefing with the FBI and Homeland Security. They were tracing the car and the explosives. And though Mike Fuller had implied, and then insisted, that I was the target, I didn't voice this to Agent Dolan. I wondered what she would come up with or if she'd tell us anything that might be helpful. David Rizzo had managed to stay on the lam from everyone, including his own parents, and he was still a wanted man, Agent Dolan said. She reiterated my obligation to inform her if he turned up again. I wasn't planning on following those orders. Now that his parents were in Canada, David could move around freely; he didn't have to protect them. "For obvious reasons, the bad guys want to find him before we do," Peg said when we were alone again in the office. Charlie thought he must be nearby, trying to contact me again, that he'd been sighted or had surfaced somewhere, and that the bomb was a warning to me from the Popovs. There was no way to corroborate this. Like so much else in an investigation, it was hypothesis, intuition. Charlie's primary interest was in solving the murders and reeling in the Popovs. We didn't know exactly what the FBI was after; it had been clear from the outset that their motivations were different. Vincent Cooper was in custody in the County Jail and there was enough evidence to hold him there without bail.

"At least we've got him," Charlie said. "What a trial this is going to be when we are done."

"If we ever get to trial," Peg said.

* * *

Andre Popov, the good son, was fat and wore two gold rings on his left hand. He looked a lot like his mother—soft , with large nearly black, slightly Asiatic eyes. He didn't resemble his brother Boris at all. Boris was lean, wiry, all muscle and bile. Andre smiled easily and spoke gently, the son who got away. Where was his mother? he asked. When he called State Police headquarters, he'd been told to see Charlie Griffith. We met him in a Japanese restaurant in Poughkeepsie—green walls, linen napkins. None of us could afford it except for Andre. Police investigators don't have a budget for power lunches, but Charlie said he'd take the money out of petty cash, his treat. We had no idea if the restaurant was secure, or if we had been followed to such an unlikely location. We wanted to see Andre on his own. Would he testify against his father? Against his brother?

"Your mother's in Canada," Charlie said simply.

"I know she is in Canada," Andre Popov said. "She sent me a postcard from Canada. Don't go to the farm, it said."

In fact, Charlie didn't know exactly where Irena Popov was as the Canadian authorities were not obliged to tell Charlie Griffith anything—her case was in the hands of Canadian immigration, he was told.

"Did you know the FBI has requested extradition?" Andre asked.

"You know more than we do," Charlie said.

"What explains your father? What explains your brother?" I asked.

"War. Opportunity. My father saw a way to get us all to America and he grabbed it. Intelligence, counter-intelligence. For a while he was working for the Soviets and the Americans. He may still be working for the Russians, or the Afghans, or the Pakistanis, or Al Qaeda, or the Americans. Who knows? It's not because he believes in anything. Boris takes advantage of our father's 'special arrangements,' with the U.S. government. I guess they still find him to be a valuable asset. I regret this."

We were near Vassar and the restaurant was filled with professors and students, a camouflage for our conversation. "Have the FBI been to see you?" Peg asked.

"They visited my office in California. I decided to come east when they told me my mother was in protective custody. But what's the point? I have to admit I am feeling discouraged."

"Someone will be held accountable," Charlie said, the most hopeful statement I'd heard in a long time.

Carol Bergman

* * *

I'd learned in the army, in PI school, and as Peg Singer's apprentice, that emotion must be restrained. Like soldiers, we plod on calmly and do our job regardless of any internal or external pressures. I'd chosen the David Rizzo case, or perhaps it had found me, I'm not sure. My mettle had been tested with every revelation, every discussion, no more so than the day David's body was found in the river near Hudson, an old town on the east side of the river, known for its landmarked facades and invisible poverty. It was hot and dusty that Indian summer day and the body was bloated like a party balloon. A couple of kids had prodded it with a stick before they realized what it was and then they got the hell out of there, barefoot, onto the baked tarmac streets and over to the police station.

Once again, Peg asked me to be death's messenger. She asked me in Charlie's presence so I couldn't bolt or cry. Somehow they knew where the Rizzos were staying. I flew up to Toronto and called them. I said I'd like to come over to see them in person if they didn't mind. "I'll be over soon," I said. Barbara's cousin opened the door and as soon as I saw her gentle face and stepped on to the runner in the vestibule, I collapsed into tears. I haven't been trained as a messenger, I thought to myself. I'm not an angel, I'm not a god in a Greek play, and I don't know how to perform this mythic act. It had been easier with Christa's mother. I didn't know or like her so I could just mouth the words and lean into her with a gesture of comfort. Tears came to my eyes then, but they didn't linger; as soon as I pulled away from the trailer park, I'd regained my composure. But this was different. David was my contemporary, we'd grown up together, and we had survived battle and returned to the landscape of our childhood. To find him again that day in the art store was, for both of us I think, a solace. We had made a plan to sketch together, a return to wholeness and sanity, a healing expedition. Sadly, it had never happened.

When David was simply missing our task had been clearly defined: find him dead or alive. The fact that there had been three brutal murders had dampened hope, but we still had hope. Now that he could not be brought back to life, I almost didn't care who the killer was exactly. What did it matter? I had failed to net David the day he broke into my house. That might have been the only chance to save him. I took all the blame for his death onto myself and I was inconsolable. Until the result of the autopsy report came in. After that, my misery turned to anger and determination.

At first, Agent Dolan wouldn't permit an autopsy. Then Mel and Barbara returned from Canada and got to work. They arrived at eleven o'clock at night, stopped at a supermarket to pick up some food, lit up the rooms in their house, and picked up the telephone. They left a message for Mike Fuller and then they called every newspaper and television station they had ever heard of. The next morning they hired a lawyer. "We want you and Peg to keep working for us until our son's killer or killers are captured," they told me. They were thinking of one person or a gang: criminals, outlaws, the Popovs, Vincent Cooper. And even though the definition of bad guy had been expanding since the FBI turned up on our turf, the Rizzos were not afraid.

It took a couple of weeks, but finally David's body was released and a forensic autopsy was performed by specially trained doctors in an operating theater. All organ systems were thoroughly examined and tissue samples taken. David Rizzo had been poisoned by a United States Army depleted uranium bullet. It was lodged—intact—in his stomach.

CHAPTER 19

There was a wake and then a service in Rhinebeck. The police had anticipated a crowd and insisted both should take place on the same day. And they were right. The whole town was there—friends, family, acquaintances, a Rizzo cousin in the National Guard about to ship out, my parents and brothers, Rosie, Charlie Griffith and Ed De Beyer. Agent Dolan was conspicuously absent.

In our small town, David Rizzo was now as famous as a head of state or a celebrity. I slipped to the side of the entrance and watched the crowd for faces that shouldn't have been there. I was still on duty, grieving, but on duty. The police had cordoned off the street. Since the bombing everyone had been on high alert as New York City had been for months—years—after the World Trade Center attack. News of our more modest explosion had reverberated throughout the valley and we were stung. It was the realization that the troubles overseas had come home to us and that there was no way to escape the collateral damage they had caused.

I spotted Christa's mother about half-way through the morning. She was dressed primly in a gray linen suit. I thought it fitting that she'd come to pay her respects. After all, David had protected and loved her daughter. I greeted her as she passed and she nodded, but we did not say anything to one another. Mel and Barbara Rizzo did not acknowledge her presence either.

For months, we had been preparing for this day, hoping it would not arrive. It was impossible to feel grief fully now that it had arrived. In fact, I hadn't been able to feel much at all since my trip to Toronto and my collapse in the hallway of Barbara's cousin's home, except in my dreams. They still told me the truth. But during the day, I was stoical, silent and alone.

Rosie took my hand and we walked inside for the service. I didn't wake up until Mel walked up to the podium. He spoke eloquently. It was unconscionable, he said, that the wars in Iraq and Afghanistan were still going on, that they had destroyed so many young lives, touched so many families. Though David's death had not taken place on the battlefield, it was a consequence of these wars. "Didn't we go to war to prevent Saddam from using weapons of mass destruction? Where did the uranium bullet that killed our son come from? The United States Army. This wasn't friendly fire, it was murder."

The audience gasped. Reporters and photographers standing against the back wall fled outside to send in their stories on their smart phones. And then the room quieted and Barbara got up to speak about her son's grace and compassion. "Some of you knew him during his younger, more troubled days," she said. "He chose to become a warrior, to fight for his country. There was only compassion in his heart. He felt too deeply."

At the house after the burial, the doors to the garden open to the fragrant air, humming birds on three sugar-filled feeders storing up for their flight south for the winter, I felt hollow and blue. Charlie put his arm around my shoulders and told me I'd done my best, I mustn't blame myself. Barbara said, "It's not your fault," Alison. I let my own pain drift away. It was hardly noticeable in the enormous tragedy of David Rizzo's death.

CHAPTER 20

It was worse in a way than anything I'd feared, the way David had died, a depleted uranium bullet in his stomach. He had died of suffocation, not radiation—that would have taken longer—but the bullet was a message from his killers: *We have the bullets. They are in the United States. Do not interrupt our black-market operation or you will get the same.*

I was having nightmares about it like I had about the young Afghan or Iranian girl in the long brown skirt. Her nationality had not been established. And for the first time in a while I thought about Anwar. I imagined his life in Baghdad as he became a man, got married, had children, if he ever lived that long.

Mike Fuller and others had reported on the use of depleted uranium bullets in Bosnia, in Serbia, in Kuwait during the Gulf War, and in Iraq by both NATO and United States forces. More than 2000 tons of these bullets had been used in the American invasion of Iraq. Few questions had been asked in Congress, fewer still internationally. Abandoned or burned-out tanks contaminated by these American-made weapons of mass destruction had become playgrounds for Iraqi children who were developing leukemia at very high rates. Now refugee camps in Jordan were filled with sick children from Syria too. And soldiers who had fought in the Gulf War had developed a "syndrome," linked to depleted uranium. I had shot more than one such bullet out of my own 30 caliber weapon contaminating whatever lay in front of us, behind us, and to either side. More than likely I and my buddies had inhaled the aerosol spray produced on impact and carried the toxic metal home inside our bodies. Considering the collateral damage we had caused to the people of occupied Iraq, it seemed like an appropriate penance. There had to be some penance. Not justice, not forgiveness, but penance. Barbara and Mel, however, were intent on justice and revelation. Not in the Christian sense, not at all. They would not rest until everything connected to David's death had been exposed and they were now more interested than ever in explanations. They had no fear, they told me, and they would not stop until their son's killers had been caught. I remembered Mike Fuller's caution months ago when he had urged me to let David tell his story before notifying his parents that he was still alive. "There are larger issues," he had said, "a greater good than one man's life." I was certain David would have agreed. Now that he was dead, his parents felt the same.

Peg and Charlie and I were still on the case, tracking down Boris Popov, keeping our eye on Vladimir, questioning Vincent Cooper, who was still in custody. He was a foot soldier, nothing more, and did what he was told. The room where he was being held was a sterile lock-down. The only decorative touches were the tattoos on his chest, arms and back, images of dragons, knives, and mayhem. They were like thumbnail action movies, or scenes of war, etched onto his sun-roughened skin. The most we could hope for was his statement that Boris Popov was his friend and that he worked for him. He had already confessed to his mother's murder.

* * *

It was the end of summer, the very end, and coming up to Labor Day. Yellow jackets feasted on the humming bird feeders and cut through the tear in my bedroom screen, a few leaves drifted onto the deck, the tomatoes were nearly all harvested, the concord grapes, the corn. It was chilly in the morning and after sunset, then intolerably hot again in the afternoon. The sun set earlier and rose later and clouds drifted faster over the mountains as the earth tipped and the winds intensified. Barbara Rizzo was in her hair salon clearing out the cobwebs. I offered to help, to keep her company, to talk. I went there to meet her every day for a week. She had a bandana on her head and her face was puffy from tears. "I even cry in my sleep," she said. We swept, we tidied. Barbara put a framed photograph of David over the mantel with two candles and fresh flowers in a small fluted vase. David was in his army uniform—handsome, upright, eager, the green beret of the Special Operations Forces cocked jauntily on his head. "Would you like a cut?" she asked. So I sat in her chair and let her cut my hair to shoulder length and then up to my ears. It reminded me of the first cut I'd had when I enlisted. I didn't like it, but I let her cut and cut. "Will you find him?" she asked, and I assured her that we would, that Boris Popov was not far away, that he was hovering somewhere near the farm on Rte. 28 and, when he surfaced, we'd get him. I didn't tell her there was no guarantee there'd ever be a trial.

It had started to rain. The rain was like a curtain behind which secrets were hidden. I had forgotten my umbrella and, as I ran to the car, I got completely wet. I dried off with an old towel I used to clean the windows and called my therapist. The windshield wipers pulsed a desperate beat in the heavy downpour. I was making plans to clamber into the mountain solo to find Boris, then head back down to the farm and mutilate Vladimir. And how different were these plans from what I had done overseas under the auspices of the United States government? I couldn't see the difference and, sitting there in my therapist's office, I can't say that my distorted thinking clarified, though I did calm down. The evidence was accumulating, the witnesses—Irena Popov, her son, Andre, even Vincent Cooper. He could turn against Boris to get a lighter sentence, life with a possibility of parole instead of life. Why had he killed his mother? "Listen, I hated the bitch even before she threatened to go to the police," he had said in his confession. Does a killer need any more reason than that to slice his mother into pieces? "Do not speak of yourself in the same breath as Vincent Cooper," my therapist said when I told her yet again about the killing fields in Iraq.

* * *

An email arrived from Mike Fuller:

Alison,

I found Christa's father in Afghanistan. His wife is not innocent.

Mike

The simplicity of the statement made me cringe. I had had an intuition, but followed it awkwardly. Later, I'd asked myself if I'd been imagining things and lost confidence in my observations. Agent Dolan had triggered my self-doubts, threatened my independent actions, and suggested I was a renegade. As for Peg and Charlie, they had lost the thread of Christa's mother's false story and let it drop. And though I couldn't forget my encounters with this odd, unemotional woman in the trailer park, I had let my suspicions drop also.

The next day, I went back to the salon to talk to Barbara. I turned over what I knew in my mind about Christa's family: mother, Iranian, father a businessman of some sort, not traveling in Japan but in Afghanistan, and doing what exactly? And Christa already in trouble with drugs in high school. "They didn't always live in the trailer park," Barbara said. "She and her husband owned a renovated Victorian near the Taconic. Then, from one day to the next, it was sold and they were living in the trailer park down in Hyde Park. David clammed up. He wouldn't say another word about Christa. I think her parents threatened him. Mel knew something was wrong and went to see them, not a good idea, but we were already feeling desperate about David's relationship with Christa. He told his parents we wanted the relationship to end, that we would take steps, if necessary. Then David went to college, and signed up. But the relationship with Christa never ended, until she was murdered."

Obvious in retrospect, this story made me sick. Barbara and Mel still held untold stories. Why? I could only attribute these lapses to shock and an amnesia that sets in as a consequence of trauma, a scrambled brain, all sequence and connection obliterated. I, too, had suffered from trauma and was working hard with my therapist to heal. It might take years she had said when I expressed impatience. "You'll learn to manage it, but it won't ever go away. It will become part of your life experience. You are already making good use of what you learned in Iraq in your personal and professional life." Compared to my super-charged emotions, the comment seemed corny. Still, I kept going back for sessions; there was no choice.

An engine idled in the parking lot behind the salon. It was the only sound I heard. The diesel fumes were strong and Barbara said, "Shut the door, will you, Alison?" So I shut the door and stood there leaning against it, my back collapsing under the weight of death and deceit. Had we known, I said to myself again, we might have been able to save Christa and David.

Of course, there was more to the story. There always is. Just as we head out the door after an interview, put on our coat and turn the doorknob, important facts surface, sometimes the most important. Psychiatrists call it "the doorknob effect." We turn around to capture unexpected sentences, retrieve the notebook we've already tucked away in our pocket, and listen again. I wasn't about to leave the salon though Barbara had probably seen my deflated expression; I'd gone on a mental walkabout. Now I was back.

"The way Mel described the scene, I knew something very ugly was going on in that family, much more than Christa's habit," Barbara continued. "Once, I had spotted Christa and her father at the Kingston Mall and the way he had her arm around her was strange, not like a father and daughter, more like lovers. I couldn't figure out where David fit into that picture and it bothered me. Mel was alarmed. That's when he decided to go to the house."

"I'll need to speak to Mel," I said, my mind still not settled into the present. I thought of a line from a poem I'd learned in grade school about pain: *We must be wicked to deserve such pain*. I had rejected this religious warning to sinners and hated the poem. I was not a sinner and most people I knew were not sinners. I wanted to change the line to say: *They must be wicked to inflict such pain.*

CHAPTER 21

I followed Barbara down to Rhinebeck. She was driving too slowly and weaving into the oncoming lane. I honked, flashed my lights, and motioned for her to pull over. I asked her if she was on medication. It hadn't occurred to me before that she might be. "I don't think you are in any shape to drive," I said. "It's okay, Alison," she said, but she refused to get out of the car. We continued slowly. This time I led the way with flashers on. It was like a funeral cortege without a body, without flowers. I made a mental note to mention Barbara's erratic driving to Mel. He was in the garden when we arrived, laid down his tools and threw some weeds into the compost pile before stepping cautiously into the house. Some people show their thoughts on their face and Mel was one of them. He didn't like gardening, but was doing it because Barbara had given it up. I said, "It's your duty to tell us everything you know." The months behind were littered with similar reprimands. I was tiring of my clients.

"I would do that if I knew who to trust," he said. "No rules, torture with impunity, criminal activity seen as helpful by our government, even necessary, to win a war. Our son wasn't killed on the battlefield, Alison."

Barbara announced dinner and asked me to stay. It would be a long night, I thought. And I wanted to call Charlie and Peg as soon as it was over. I took out my notebook and put it on the table in front of me. This was not a social call or a bereavement visit. We were back at work and I wanted my note-taking to be as meticulous as Peg's. Recording everyone's words was also a way of paying attention and controlling my baser impulses. Reviewing the notes was a different process and always involved brainstorming with Peg and Charlie. I couldn't do it on my own. "Christa's father tried to trap David into criminal activity without success. I'm convinced of that," Mel began.

I hoped the Popovs name would come up as Mel spoke. Had they lived in the area for a long time?

Mel got up to pull the curtains on the sliding glass doors that led to the garden. Night had fallen and the sensation of someone prowling had not abated. Headlights flashing off the road bounced away into the woods. They were fairly constant. Mel continued, "I don't know for sure what Christa's parents were doing though I knew it was illegal. I decided to keep it simple the day I went to the house, just to talk to them about Christa. I'm a psychologist, I said. I could help you arrange an intervention. David would help."

"David wasn't on drugs?"

"He never did the hard stuff," Barbara said.

"So how did Christa's father respond to your offer?"

"He blew me off. He said he wasn't interested and I should mind my own business. He swore. He raged. Christa came out to see what was going on. He put his arm around her shoulders and said, 'You're okay aren't you, baby?' Her eyelids were drooping; she was high. It all flashed in front of me, how he was using her, how he was the one who had gotten his daughter hooked. I told David about it but all he said was, 'I've got to hang in and save her, Dad.' He was in a lot of pain over Christa. And he was in so deep with her and that family. When he went off to college we thought his involvement might end, but it didn't."

Mel spoke like a man with professional authority, an adviser who expected to be heeded. He had failed with his own son and I could sense disappointment and embarrassment in his voice. Why hadn't David listened to him? Why had he signed up after college? Somewhere, in some direction, there was an answer to David's murder, Mel said. He must have died for something. I reached out my hand for the salt, the bowl of packaged stale parmesan. Nothing that Barbara had prepared had any flavor; it was already my second helping of the cheese. She said, "You can use your influence, Alison." So I told her she could count on me to stay with the case until Boris Popov was in custody, but that I had no influence as to any final outcome. None of us did.

"We wouldn't want to ask you to do more than you can do," Mel said.

He was always interpreting Barbara's comments which often, these days, did not make sense. Moodiness descended. Why bother explaining again the constraints of the Patriot Act, the presence of the FBI? There didn't seem any point.

"We won't let Boris Popov escape," I said. "We have a good team. The State troopers are terrific. We will get him."

"I would shoot him myself," Barbara said, her voice trailing off as she loaded the dishwasher. Mel got up to help her as I cleared the table and tried to remember what else I had wanted to ask Mel about his conversation with Christa's parents.

"What did Christa's mother say?" I asked.

"She was mostly quiet," Mel said. "But she was not blind."

I groped through my memory for that line. It was from Jane Austen.

CHAPTER 22

I called Peg. I called Charlie. Though it was late, past 10 p.m., we decided to meet in Charlie's office. No murderer should be allowed to benefit from his crime, but what if these crimes are camouflaged by war-time action or espionage, Charlie asked, what then? What is local law enforcement to do? None of us had expected the presence of the FBI, or the confusion of a paid spy-master covering for a son, or a mother whose criminal allegiances trumped her parental obligations. We still couldn't figure out how Christa's parents fit into the scenario and we might have to wait to find out, or might never find out. We were all tired, struggling with the puzzle. Irena Popov had been extradited and was in FBI custody. Charlie had found out about it from her son, Andre, who had received a call from Agent Dolan's office to say his mother was safe. Safe. What did that mean? Dolan hadn't had the courtesy to phone Charlie Griffith directly, another end-play that undermined our investigation, for some greater good, Peg quipped. They've got my mother and won't let me speak to her," Andre had said. "God knows what they will do with her or where they will send her for interrogation."

"What did our trip to Canada accomplish?" Peg asked. "We alienated Agent Dolan and got a couple of lines in an obscure Canadian newspaper that no one outside of Canada reads. When the U.S. government tells the Canadian government to shut up, they shut up."

I piled some cushions onto the floor and told Charlie I'd spend the night if he thought it would do any good. "I just need to rest a bit," I said. And then I drifted off. I woke to the sunrise, a slash of orange against a cloudless, cobalt sky. Though no rain was in the forecast, it smelled like rain. Birds were singing—they are always singing—and I could hear someone shuffling along the hallway. It was only then I realized where I was. I had been disoriented every night of my two deployments, sleeping rough in the field or back at base, I never knew exactly where I was when I woke up. And in the few seconds it took to get my bearings, I groped my way into consciousness against the darkness of my depleted spirit. But I wasn't overseas anymore; I was in Charlie Griffith's office.

I got up and stretched, straightened my clothes, found the bathroom. When I returned, Charlie was there. It was good to see him. "I see you're still here. We didn't want to wake you as we left," he said.

"What did you decide last night?"

"We're going to get a search warrant and surprise Christa's mother. Have you heard from Mike Fuller? Our only hope is to get something into the newspapers."

"He'll be back soon, or soon enough," I said, confident that he'd be beyond reliable in his determination to get the story. I couldn't foresee anything that might go wrong except a bullet in his head. And he'd sent whatever he had to his editors electronically as he went along with his investigation. If he couldn't write it, someone else would write it in his stead. "None of us are indispensable," he had said to me often. He was including me.

"Do you think there'll be any shooting down at the trailer?" I asked Charlie. I didn't want to be around any shooting. I hadn't slept well and my head was pounding.

"Go get yourself some breakfast. The warrant should be in by the time you come back. Peg's on her way."

So I walked into town. Students were returning from the summer break, term starting, and the streets were already busy with cars filled to overflowing with suitcases, bundles, desk lamps and skateboards. It was already crowded and noisy at the diner by 8 a.m. But there was no place else open at that hour so I grabbed a paper and sat down at the counter, ordered some poached eggs, a coffee. I couldn't concentrate on the news. I looked up and saw Sergeant Ed De Beyer. I had assumed his grandmother's locket was back in its box and in his pocket as we evacuated, and that would be the end of our relationship. I hoped we could be friends, but I hadn't called him to apologize, or offered to meet again to apologize, after our interrupted evening together. I didn't feel like talking now so I ignored him and tried to read the newspaper. It wasn't a mature thing to do, but that's what I did.

* * *

I could see a silhouette behind the curtains as we pulled in, a woman watching television. I don't think she realized we were there. Troopers were stacked behind us on Rte. 9 and they'd set up a detour. It was dusk and the birds I'd heard chirping in the morning were already bedding down for the night. My fear lifted as I said to myself: I'm doing this for David.

The well-groomed woman sat her in sanitized living room sewing the hem on a skirt. She was watching *Lonesome Dove*. "I like those two actors," Peg said as we walked in. The door had been open as though someone was expecting guests and didn't want to be disturbed when they arrived. "Read the book, Charlie?" Peg asked as she sat down. "The book is better," Charlie said.

I stepped around the glass-topped table in front of the television, picked up the remote, and flicked it off. Charlie handed Christa's mother the search warrant. She put it on the table and kept on sewing.

"You had us fooled," Peg said. "That demure exterior, the carefully constructed living space, the story you told about Christa, your missing husband, your job at the Culinary Institute. We're going to search your trailer." Charlie stepped outside and radioed the troopers to begin. Their movements under the trailer rocked the thin-walled metal cabin.

"I've done nothing. You'll find nothing," she said quickly, three times.

"At the very least, you lied to us," I said, "and withheld information."

"I've done nothing wrong."

"You need to pay attention," Mrs. Woolf, Peg said.

"I don't have to talk to you. I want to call my lawyer."

As the troopers rummaged around us, the air was filled with dust mites and gnats.

"Are you a pious person?" I asked.

"What do you mean?"

"If you're a pious person, I'd say a few Inshallahs right now."

"That's how little you know," Mrs. Woolf said disdainfully. That accent again. I'd heard it slip off the throats of the Iranians in Iraq. They spoke Farsi—not Arabic—and so they were obvious when they turned up because they needed translators. The Iran-Iraq war had lasted eight miserable years in the 1980s. It was a war that has been compared to World War I with soldiers in trenches and the use of mustard gas. Half a million soldiers as well as civilians died, many more were injured. What did these overtures between former enemies signify? And what was the young Farsi-speaking girl—for I was sure, now, that she was Iranian—doing in the Popov's house? Had Christa's parents put her there?

"If you knew all I know, you'd see my point of view," Mrs. Woolf said.

"It'd take a lot of talking to persuade us of that," Charlie said.

There was some scuffling on the shallow steps and then a trooper called to Charlie to come outside. Peg followed, I stayed inside. We could easily see and hear what was going on as the troopers pulled out bricks of heroin wrapped in plastic bags inside of burlap bags from the Popov's farm. I said, "I'm surprised you didn't get high just sitting here." I stood up and blocked the doorway but Mrs. Farideh Woolf stayed seated, expressionless, as she had always been. I stepped away from the door and told her to stand up and prepare herself for arrest. Within minutes she was in the back seat of Charlie's car. She lowered her head onto her chest, her hands cuffed behind her.

CHAPTER 23

"I'm glad you invited me," Rosie said. "It's such a hot day. I hate being alone on holiday weekends."

We were at the Ulster County Pool just outside of New Paltz, Labor Day Sunday, and the pool was crowded. There were honky-tonk sounds from the Fair Grounds next door, children shrieking, lifeguards blowing their whistles, mothers and fathers shouting at their kids to do this and not do that. We headed for the grassy knoll near the half-Olympic lap-lane and laid out towels and coolers. One lifeguard's chair was to our left near the diving board, another was at the far end of the lap lane, three more at other locations. I entered the lap lane, cap and goggles so tight I could only hear the thumping of my own heart and the swish of water in my wake. I glanced up at the cloudless sky, a hawk circling. The diving board was over my left shoulder.

I recognized Boris Popov after the first flip turn. Now the diving board was over my right shoulder. I swam faster and flipped again. There he was, ready to dive off the high board. He wore a bright red bikini that only diving champions or Europeans wear. I didn't stop swimming until his body soared off the board landing just feet from my head. Then I kept going and so did he. Up and down he went as I swam my laps on the other side of the barrier separating the diving area from the lap lane. Even with my head in the water, I was watching him as he pierced the water and came up for air. No one seemed to be with him. A small bundle of clothes and a towel were piled near the base of the diving board. He went over now and again to check his cell phone. Then he took another dive, and another. He was a good diver, more than an amateur. Broad shoulders, I thought. How many bones has this man crushed?

I got out of the pool at the far end, popped my goggles on top of my cap, but left the cap on, a disguise of sorts. Rosie was on her back roasting in the strong sun. She was a beach baby. I didn't want to tell her it wasn't going to be a relaxing Sunday after all.

"You're dripping on me, Alison," she said.

"Don't move, stay right there. I've got to make a phone call. Then I'm going to come back and get you. Gather your belongings slowly, no sudden movements, and take mine while you're at it."

"What's going on?"

"I'll tell you later," I said, grabbing my phone and walking into the shade of the pavilion which had a canteen and dressing rooms.

I remembered Iraq, how the sun had made me slow. There was no place to swim there but all I could think about in the Humvee was swimming. I obsessed about water and shade and trees while I was in Iraq. The most beautiful wild flowers grow along the road there, huge purple flowers with leaves like thistles. I wanted to pick them, or dig them up and take them back to base and replant them in clay pots, but that would have been too dangerous. I could not keep my mind steady as I walked to the pavilion thinking of those flowers. Rosie could have helped me snap out of it, but I had ignored Rosie. And now I felt as though I was on my own, a ridiculous delusion.

"Griffith here," Charlie said as he answered the phone. He sounded British sometimes, an endearing trait.

"I'm at the Ulster County Pool, Charlie, and guess who's here doing his diving routine—Boris Popov. I'm watching him now.

Some kids are asking him questions, asking him to do another dive. That might keep him around for a few more minutes.

"On it, Alison. Stay put, keep your phone on."

"Don't run any sirens. He's in and out of the water, his back to the parking lot. I don't think he'll see the patrol cars if they slide in behind the pavilion."

"He'll be on the lookout, Alison. "He's well trained."

"Maybe he's gone completely feral. He had the nerve to come down here and spend a pleasant afternoon in the open. He may be so pathological he thinks he's invulnerable. "

"I've seen that before," Charlie said.

"Too many times."

"I'm worried about the crowd, Alison. The place must be full of kids."

"I don't think we can evacuate without tipping him off."

"He's canny," Charlie said.

My confidence had returned and I was sure and steady. It was the scent of battle, adrenalin pumping. Boris Popov was insane to think he could escape.

"Let's stay a bit longer," I said to Rosie. "I'd like to swim again."

I didn't want her to know what was happening, not just yet.

I knew that I could keep my eye on things in the pool and sprint to the side when the action started. I could already see the blue and yellow State Police SUV's through the gaps in the fence behind the canteen. The troopers would stay in their vehicles waiting for orders, windows shut against the heat, their radios set to low volume.

I swam one lap and then another, until a young man in a bathing suit walked over to Boris and offered his hand in congratulation. Boris broke a smile. He had some teeth missing and his nose was fighter flattened. I didn't think the fights had taken place in any ring. I took my time making a turn and looked over the grounds. The kids, maybe ten of them now, were clamoring for Boris to show them some tricks. He headed up the ladder as the young man waited a beat and then followed him up. He was Charlie's undercover. Popov turned around, looked out into the lot, and saw the patrol cars. He only had two choices: Get past the cop coming up the ladder behind him or dive into the water. I scrambled out of the pool and herded as many people as I could away from the green verge around the diving board and then out through the gate. Other troopers and then the sheriff arrived and evacuated everyone else—except Rosie—who was still on her beach towel. I hadn't told her what to do and she was watching me closely.

The cop didn't make it to the top before Boris flew off the board. He swam like crazy, clambered out, and grabbed Rosie, but he had no weapon. Rosie stuck her hand into his ribs and locked his head firmly. The drama was over.

* * *

We walked into the interrogation room together—Charlie, Peg and I. Charlie took out his revolver and put it on the table

"That's against regulations," Boris Popov said.

"I'm celebrating," Charlie said.

"Charlie," Peg said quietly.

"I have nothing against you," Boris Popov said. "All you need to know is this: David was a fool, Christa was my girl when he was still overseas, and then she turned on me. That's all you need to know."

"I don't expect you to talk straight, Popov, but do me a favor and don't refer to me personally," Charlie said.

"Very well, I won't," Popov said.

He closed his eyes and seemed to be asleep for a while. I went outside into the parking lot. The uneasy feeling had not dissipated with the events of the day or Boris Popov's arrest. Christa had been Boris Popov's girl—or so he said, but why should we believe him, I thought. David was devoted to Christa; he had tried to save her.

* * *

Two days later, Peg and I drove down to Newburgh to see Agent Dolan in her new office. We still represented the Rizzo family. We wanted to know why the FBI hadn't shown any interest in our arrest and interrogation of Boris Popov. We hadn't heard a word from them. Agent Dolan said, "I bet Labor Day Sunday was the best day you've had in a long time, Ms. Singer."

"I guess I was dreaming," Peg said. "And Boris Popov's arrest never happened."

Agent Dolan said. "I'd take my time if I were you. Boris Popov was probably framed. That's all you need to know; the rest is classified."

"That's bullshit," I said. "You knew he wouldn't talk. He's got some kind of immunity, right?"

My voice quivered slightly from frustration and rage. I couldn't accept Agent Dolan's account and it wasn't just because it was a lie. I wanted her to take back what she had said and step onto our side, a false hope if ever there was one. She liked her job too much and the clout she carried with it. I wasn't tough enough to beat her at this game.

"Don't let's hear any more about this, Ms. Jenkins, Ms. Singer. Your investigation is over."

"Maybe so," I said. "Or maybe not," Peg said.

And then we left. There was nothing more to say.

* * *

There was an orchard by the side of the road and I wanted to stop there before going back to the office. The trees were loaded with ripening apples and when I looked into the branches they were as twisted as my deranged thoughts. I hated Agent Dolan. Peg put her hand on my shoulder and we walked back and forth across the rows of trees. I said, "I've forgotten the meaning of the word justice," and Peg said, "You know what it means, Alison. You'll always know what it means."

I wanted it to snow. I wanted to go skiing. I hoped no one else would get killed anywhere near Ulster or Dutchess County in the near future because I didn't have the wisdom, or the energy, or the intuition to help solve another murder and then watch the murderer walk away under escort of the United States government. I hoped that when Boris Popov was released—because I was sure he would be—that he'd get shot in Baghdad, or Basra, or Kurdistan, or Kabul, or Beirut, or Damascus, his body chopped up for dog food though I wouldn't even wish dogs such poison.

EPILOGUE

There was a shallow stream running over driftwood and lichen-covered rocks at the bottom of Mike Fuller's property. I sat down on the bank and took off my shoes. The water was ice cold; it never warmed up in the mountains. It was luxurious sitting there, without a past or a future. But the sensation of peace soon evaporated. I thought of Christa and David, their bodies, their youth, their wasted lives. I thought of the young, kidnapped Iranian girl, of Vincent Cooper's mother. I put my shoes back on and walked to the front of the house. My feet were wet. Mike sat outside with me while I dried them off. I stayed for a week because there didn't seem to be any place else for me to go. I watched Mike work, I cooked, and I sat on the porch and rocked on his rocker. I kept my gun loaded.

A few weeks later, Mike Fuller's articles began to appear in newspapers and on websites all over the world. They appeared in four installments and punctuated the election season. American personnel, still in uniform, were running arms, drugs, and girls, recruiting local warlords, getting paid in cash from everyone. Christa's father was the godfather of the operation, Boris Popov its pearly prince, his father, Vladimir, its court jester. David Rizzo's name was mentioned only once as the soldier who tried to save a young Iranian girl smuggled into Iraq as a sex slave and then brought to the United States in an army transport plane with five others. He had tried to stop the trafficking and he had encouraged more than one of his comrades to confess to their commanders except that one or two of them were also involved in the lucrative enterprise. Mike Fuller named them. And then he exposed the FBI and the government's interest in the case. It was the depleted uranium bullets they were mostly worried about. Too many had gone missing.

None of these articles ended the wars in Iraq or Afghanistan or Syria, but we got a new president who awarded David Rizzo a posthumous Medal of Honor. Barbara added it to the shrine in her salon and lit candles every day. She kept the flowers fresh in the fluted vase. Mel printed a sign which said: *David Rizzo, an American hero, R.I.P.*

ABOUT THE AUTHOR

C arol Bergman is a journalist whose articles, essays, and interviews have appeared in *The New York Times, Cosmopolitan,* and *Salon.com.* Her essay, "Objects of Desire" was nominated for the Pushcart Prize; her short stories have appeared in many literary magazines. She is the author of biographies of Mae West and Sidney Poitier, a memoir, *Searching for Fritzi,* two books of novellas, *Sitting for Klimt* and *Water Baby* and a novel, *What Returns to Us.* She compiled and edited *Another Day in Paradise; International Humanitarian Workers Tell Their Stories,* nominated for the J. Anthony Lukas Book Prize. She lives in New Paltz, New York and teaches writing at New York University and at the SUNY Ulster Writing Center.

www.carolbergman.net

With thanks...
to my husband, Jim, and daughter, Chloe,
and to my mother who loved murder
mysteries and political thrillers and was
interested in the evolution of this book
to the end of her long, cultured life.

Made in the USA
Middletown, DE
27 July 2019